CW01650394

THE RULE OF WRATH

ALSO BY ANDY NOWICKI

Considering Suicide

The Columbine Pilgrim

The Doctor and the Heretic and Other Stories

Under the Nihil

Heart Killer

Lost Violent Souls

Beauty and the Least

This Malignant Mirage

Confessions of a Would-Be Wanker

Notes Before Death

Conspiracy, Compliance, Control, and Defiance

Meta-#Pizzagate

Ruminations of a Low-Status Male

Ravages of the "Rough Beast"

A Final Solution to the Incel Problem

The Insurrectionist

Muze

The Rule of Wrath

Andy Nowicki

Sheridan, WY
Terror House Press
2024

Copyright © 2024 Terror House Press, LLC.

All rights reserved. No part of this book may be reproduced or utilized in any form or by any means (whether electronic or mechanical), including photocopying, recording, or by any information storage and retrieval system without the prior written permission of the publisher, except in the case of brief quotations embodied in critical reviews and certain other noncommercial uses permitted by copyright law.

This is a work of fiction. Names, characters, businesses, events, and incidents are the products of the author's imagination. Any resemblance to actual persons, living or dead, or actual events is purely coincidental.

ISBN 978-1-951897-91-8

EDITOR

Matt Forney (mattforney.com)

LAYOUT AND COVER DESIGN

Matt Lawrence (mattlawrence.net)

TERROR HOUSE PRESS, LLC

terrorhousepress.com

The throng which gathered for the event was in collective good spirits, in spite of the bank of storm clouds which had gathered overhead. The prevailing mood was: *if it rains and we get soaked, so what?* The joy of just being there, of hearing his sweet melodic voice, of seeing his lovely face, at once stern yet somehow also possessed of an apple-cheeked innocence, made it all worthwhile, and then some.

No prior registration was required for attendance, so entrance was "first come, first seated." The hours leading up to the rally were chaotic indeed, a "logistical nightmare," in the words of one Phazer Stadium manager, who, along with her fellow employees, had the task to ensure that the facility was not filled to overcapacity (to the point, that is, where anyone would be in danger of getting trampled or otherwise harmed), while at the same time meeting their contractual agreement with the Crumple campaign, to the effect that no one would be turned away unless capacity were truly achieved. Crumple's lawyers had played hardball on that last detail, and the clout they wielded (Crumple himself having amassed such a passionate following across the country) meant that Phazer could get some serious bad press, and possibly a lawsuit or two, if they didn't honor Crumple's demand that "the people not be denied or prevented from attending the event, barring circumstances which would seriously hamper their safety."

No specific number was given regarding what constituted "capacity." The stadium seated around 80,000, but those who chose to stand on the field (to be closer to the object of their adoration) accounted for an additional 25 to 30,000. Thousands more gathered outside of the edifice to watch their beloved leader communicate his message of "justice through unity" to his faithful adherents.

As "showtime" approached, the skies correspondingly darkened, until faint peals of thunder could be heard in the echoing distance. One couldn't escape the sensation that the heavens themselves were providing an orchestral introduction to this, a visitation from one sent from the starry climes, paying a visitation in order to remind the assembled seekers of the way back to that which had been lost. In each individual mind of those in attendance, this "lost" quality assumed a different aspect. For most, it was something entirely inchoate, something they could scarcely grasp, much less articulate to themselves, much less explain to others. But it remained there, deeply rooted in their consciousness, waiting to be summoned to the surface at the given time.

The "opening act," as it were, was an unassuming acoustic guitar playing crooner, clad in a Dylan-like ensemble: vest, overcoat, and stonewashed jeans. The crowd applauded politely through his first few songs, covers of standard upbeat rock and folk numbers, with a couple of gospel numbers thrown in for good measure. But then a subtle shift occurred, barely perceptible at first. The singer's aspect became somehow bigger, more imposing, and more commanding. He spoke for the first time:

"We've heard a lot about the 'good old days.' Are y'all ready for some good new days? How does that sound to y'all?"

A hearty cheer went up at this sentiment, "a consummation devoutly to be wished," one gathered. Immediately the minstrel launched into a rendition of "G.O.D. (Good Old Days)" by Fastball, and his voice assumed a wailing, even melancholy tinge:

"I've been thinking of the good old days
Decorated in a candy glaze
I've been climbing up the walls again
Living with a memory that might have been
So pick me up on a weekday night
We'll get together and ride around in the black and white"

These words, general though they were, aroused in nearly every spectator the same familiar longing. Many a tear duct moistened obediently, and numberless sighs involuntarily heaved within thousands of breasts. Then, upon concluding this tune, the jester in jeans smiled impishly and shouted, "So are y'all finally ready to meet the man?" This utterance, met by the expected roar of the assembled throng, prompted the minstrel to launch into another tune from the same album, whose lyrics seemed especially charged with significance for this specific occasion:

I got a warm fuzzy feeling when I saw you on TV, you were wearing a piece of me

And it breaks my heart to look around and see the unimpressed

Who can't believe the emperor is dressed

But with you up there to light the way, I can wear a smile as I survey

Their faces in the dark, waiting for you to hit one out of the park!

What are we gonna use to fill these empty spaces?

When they see her in the crowd, will you make your momma proud?

She can turn around and see the faces looking at her son

Climbing his way up to number one, scratching his way up to number one!

Then: "Ladies and gentlemen, the mother of the next president of the United States, Eveline Agatha Crumple!"

The minstrel hopped and skipped over to meet the majestically-robed woman who now emerged from the margins of the stage. He bowed, kissed her hand, and knelt before her in a comedic parody of extreme reverence. She returned the favor, wagging a finger at him, as if to admonish the minstrel for his sauciness, but with a wide grin all the while, indicating that she was indeed in on the joke. She embraced him like a long-lost friend, then as the latter leapt out of view, she assumed his former position center-stage.

The crowd's applause, cheers, hoots, hollers, and whistles went on for nearly half a minute. But Eveline knew better than to let the adulation for her run too long, lest she seem desirous to steal the spotlight from her beloved son, who was, after all, the one whom everyone really had come to see. She put up a hand, indicating in a supremely regal gesture for the assembled throng to pipe down. The throng, as one, obeyed, and fell silent.

"Thank you so much for coming out tonight. What a crowd!" she enthused, eliciting another cheer as the assembled throng acknowledged its gracious acceptance her gracious words.

What happened next had to be seen to be believed. In some ineffable way, Eveline's appearance transitioned from that of a beaming, ecstatic woman to that of a lady in mourning. Yet in this abrupt metamorphosis, she became positively radiant. Many in attendance sighed in awe, as if witnessing a divine apparition. Even those near the back picked up on this change, thanks to the Jumbotron screen; many a heart skipped, many a chest was clutched. With collective baited breath, they awaited her words:

"21 years ago, on this very day, I suffered the saddest, most tragic day of my life."

She spoke into the microphone in little more than a whisper, but the now utterly silent crowd heard every word, articulated with meticulous precision. They more than heard, in fact; rather, her words resonated in their souls. They sat in awe, eager to consume every morsel of her message.

"Twenty-one years ago was also the happiest, most joyous day of my life," she continued, though her face still signified sorrow. "It was the day… the day my dear departed husband, Evan Crumple, and I, made love and conceived my son…"

Shocking and intimate, perhaps excessively intimate, as this revelation was, nobody groaned or giggled with embarrassment. Instead, the assembled throng came to an identical understanding: they were indeed privileged to hear these words; sacred truth was unfolding before their eyes, something like a Nativity story was being related to them.

"Then, later that same day, Evan was…senselessly lost." She little needed to elaborate; everyone by now knew how Crumple, a bright and shining star in the Senate who sought to bring decency back to government and to eliminate corruption, was killed in an automobile accident involving an aide who was a drunk driver, and who was later found to be an unstable, perhaps schizophrenic man. That aide's name was now long forgotten, but the legend of Evan Crumple lived on; he was valorized as an idealist who was tragically plucked from the world in the prime of his career, just as he was on the precipice of doing much good. Statues of Evan Crumple had sprung up in many places across the country. In every image, the martyred hero was displayed as a man of profoundly wise character, with a twinkle of whimsy in his eye. Though not handsome, Crumple's stout figure was usually rendered as avuncular; he was the sort of public figure who had been "relatable," while at the same time seeming, paradoxically, "larger than life."

"I said, a moment ago, that Evan's death was senseless, but in truth, it was not at all senseless. It happened, it turns out, at just the right time. For before he passed on, he planted that needful seed into my waiting womb..." Here she paused, and sighed with great emotion, as if experiencing that moment of conception all over again. Her eyes closed and she shuddered with conspicuous delectation, recalling the sensation of new life awakening within her. Again, the rapt audience, far from being put off by the brazenness of her manner of expression, responded with a sense of awe: the tragic departure of the father coincided with the nativity of the one whose life would change everything indelibly.

Presently, Eveline opened her eyes again, her face animated with something like post-coital contentment. She ran her finger through her lustrous raven hair; she displayed no gray whatsoever and indeed looked nearly two decades younger than her 55 year-old frame. Many had remarked upon her remarkably youthful appearance and not a few had noticed her still quite potent sex appeal. What on Earth, or elsewhere, was her secret?

Then, as if on cue, a peal of thunder roared forth from the heavens. All was still. Eveline remained unfazed.

"Nine months later, he came forth. From the first time I was set alight by the spark of his being, I knew that my son was special. When he was born, and I saw him, looked into his bright little eyes, my initial feelings were only confirmed. And for every single moment of his life afterwards, the way I felt, when I first felt him quicken inside me, then when I witnessed his arrival into the world, I have become all the more convinced that this boy, this man, this extraordinary person, my son, will change the course of the world!"

The crowd roared in avid agreement, and another peal of thunder rang out, indicating the seeming enthusiastic consent of the heavens.

"If every tongue were still, the stones themselves would cry out!" she declared. "The Earth itself would yell for our next leader, my dear son, the fruit of the sweet loins of my dear, departed husband, Mr. Evan Aaron Crumple Junior!"

A few discerning observers of the proceedings were struck by Eveline's choice of words: "leader," rather than "president." Yet even those who applied discernment to this event (and there were but a few who were not overcome by a frenzy of emotion which approached enrapturement) would have guessed that Eveline Agatha Crumple, widow of the late Senator Evan Crumple and mother of presidential aspirant Evan Aaron Crumple, had baldfacedly *lied* in the intimate details she had shared. None, not even the most skeptical, would have guessed that, shockingly enough, the man now taking the stage to an explosion of full-throated cheers from thousands of followers, in fact possessed a wholly divergent paternal origin than that which had just been professed by his lovely, passionate, and devoted mother.

Evan Jr. now strode into view, dressed in an elegant sweater vest and charcoal-colored corduroy trousers. Unlike his ostensible father, Evan Jr. was tall, slender, and arrestingly handsome. He flashed a killer smile, which dazzled even as it disarmed, for it betrayed both confidence and a sort of secret shyness, a half-hidden vulnerability. At age 20 (around three months shy of 21, as had been earlier established by the less than delicate revelations of his mother), he was in the full flower of youth, a glorious specimen to behold. Women sighed and swooned, while men saw in him the son they wished they'd had, or the brother they'd always wanted. He waved jovially to the throng, as if happily greeting close friends after coming home from a long trip. Eveline hugged him hard, kissed him briefly on the lips and kicked a stockinged leg into the air with a sly, mischievous smirk, before sashaying off into the wings. Evan winced comedically at his mother's unrestrained and indulgent gesture, and a supportive laugh ripped through the packed colosseum.

"They said we couldn't do it!" he declared. "Were they right?"

"Nooooooooooooo!" yelled nearly 100,000 strong in immediate response, knowing instinctively the context meant by the adored speaker.

"They said, 'He's too young! The law says it is forbidden. The law says he must be 35!' Did that stop us?"

"Noooooooooooo!" came the lusty response.

"Fuck no, that didn't stop us!" Evan exulted. "We just got them to change that stupid law, didn't we?"

The crowd roared, and another thunderclap rang out.

"We showed them just what 'We the people' means, didn't we? It doesn't mean, 'They, the government,' it means 'We the people.' WE, not THEY!"

Now the throng ecstatically launched into an extended parroting of this newly-minted phrase: *"We not they, we not they, we not they, we not they!"*

As this mantra echoed through Phazer Stadium, its coiner nodded, flashing a mischievous smile quite resembling that of his mother.

"And speaking of 'they,'" he went on. "And we all know who 'they' are, don't we? *They* are the ones who think they have the right to rule the rest of us. *They* want us to stay in our place. *They* want us to sit down and shut up…and *they* sure have run us through the ringer, haven't they?"

His jaw had now set in that flint-like expression of anger and disgust. Handsome and elegantly dapper though he was, at moments like these Evan Jr. looked positively terrifying, like a beast stalking its prey in the wilderness. His adherents, however, were not put off in the least, for they knew he stalked on their behalf, and hunted those whom they hated, loathed, and feared.

"What have the past two decades brought us? Phony pandemics? Wars? Food shortages? 'Oh, we're doing our best,' they say. 'Just do as we say! First they say, 'stay indoors until we tell you do come out, the virus is too dangerous!' 'Then they say, 'Get this shot, even though it's an experimental vaccine that might kill you, or else you will lose your job…' then, 'Send your sons and daughters off to Eastern Europe or Northern Asia to fight in wars that have nothing to do with them, or you, and anyone, other than the obscenely rich criminals who run this corrupt system. Then they said, 'Collect these rations, or we will not permit you to feed your family, because the economy has crashed and we can do nothing about it…nothing they could do about it? The economic downturn sure wasn't hurting them, was it? We all saw the videos of them, those obscene oligarchs, indulging in their fancy parties, sailing their luxury yachts, gathering in filthy profligacy at their conferences to discuss their plans for the fate of humanity, while the rest of us struggled to pay our bills, struggled to put gas in our cars, struggled to eat, struggled to live!"

By now, the throng's collective psyche had been catapulted into an orgy of anger and indignation. They roared, they snarled, they stomped, they booed and whistled, all to signify their hatred and contempt for the nefarious machinations exercised against them by the forces invoked by the man who strode before them like a ravening lion out for blood.

"*They!*" he exclaimed. "*They* want us at each others' throats. *They* want us devouring each other, every election season! Every four years, they set us against each other…they want our anger to be expressed laterally. But we must grow wise, friends. It is misdirection. They strike us from above, then induce us to point fingers at one another, to attack and even kill each other. But it is *they* that should pay, not us! *They,* not us!"

"*They, not us, they not us, they not us, they not us, they not us!*" The throng had once again been provoked to engage a lusty, full-throated, vigorous chant. Evan let them carry on for nearly the span of a minute, then, as soon as the roar began to show signs of dying down, he essayed forward.

"But *we,* not *they,* shall prevail!" he declared. "Because they know by now that their time is running out!" He turned his head up, seeming now to address a hidden group of fearful eyes watching him from various places of prominence. "Do you hear my words, *Phazer??* You, the very ones who named this stadium, who are responsible for forcing millions of people to go to their deaths, along with the rest of your pharmaceutical robber baron cronies. You will pay for your crimes! We, the people, will see to that!"

The crowd again roared, hooted, and hollered.

"Do you hear me, *military-industrial corporate complex,* you who have sent so many of our young into the meat grinder of eternal war? Do you hear us? You will not divide us any longer. We are united, and we are coming for you! All you sitting in high places, *it's all gonna fall on you!*"

Evan in fact improvised the last statement, the known lyric from a once-popular song, still alive in the consciousness of the masses, or at least what was left of the masses following the catastrophes that had engulfed so much of the nation (as well as the world) in the past few decades.

"You tried to replace us, you *ghouls,* you *thugs,* you *demons.* But you have failed. We are still here! You won't replace us, *we will replace you!*"

Another thunderclap issued forth at that moment, followed by a flash of lightening. But the men and women present in the stadium did not quail or cringe; instead, the on-cue heavenly pyrotechnics only served to set their souls ablaze with wrathful determination. They now chanted, *"We will replace you, we will replace you, we will replace you!"* The frenzy of the throng had by now exploded forth like a supernova of hyper-focused hatred; this fire was not in the least dampened when seconds later the skies finally opened and dumped a fateful deluge upon the faithful in assemblage. The downpour did not diminish their enthusiasm one whit: though soaking wet within seconds they continued to chant and cheer, their eyes smoldering with unquenched wrath.

"The storm… is here! Thank you my friends. *Onward to victory!*"

Evan, now drenched himself, stood unashamedly before his fans and followers. He smiled with determination and defiance, and raised his arms high with each fist tightly clenched, displaying uninhibited verve. His tall, lean, lithe body stretched inexorably heavenward; to those in attendance, he seemed to be the true rainmaker, the orchestrator of the storm, the one for whom the thunder enthusiastically clapped and the lightening appreciatively flashed.

Moments later, the deafening roar of the throng still reverberating thrillingly against his eardrums, Evan entered his trailer, accompanied by two burly security men. He politely asked them to leave, and they obediently scattered from his sight. Left alone, Evan promptly removed his soaking wet clothes, flung them to the floor, grabbed a towel from atop a nearby dresser, and sat naked on the bunk in his trailer, its bedding still unmade.

He attempted to clear his mind, to put away the exultation that he always felt after events like these. The crowds had only been building, slowly but steadily, throughout his campaign, but lately things had gotten to the point where the fanaticism of the assemblages which followed him around had become a little frightening. It gave him the impression, when he thought about it, of wildfire, burning with a ferocity that even fire itself never really assumes, even when at its most extreme state of lethal flammability. The fire that he saw, that he felt, both within him and without him, was one that would surely burn down the world, would never be consumed, would rage throughout eternity…was it, then, Hell that he was bringing? But none of the words he spoke were untrue; in fact, he strongly believed his message to be a deeply righteous one. How could a righteous source bring Hell, whose most salient characteristic was its being located in the realm of the incorrigibly wicked?

Try as he may, Evan could not reconcile these disparate impressions; they seemed, in fact, to self-contradict at a basic level. Though not a religious man, or rather, not a man who had ever given religion much thought, he possessed a visceral, one might even say primal, sense of good and evil. That both were quite real was a principle about which he had never harbored the least speck of doubt. Indeed, he saw himself as a man on a mission, and he was, it may be said, a "true believer"; though he knew how to be both a showman and a shaman to further his cause, there was not a speck of cynicism within him. So this vision he had, of an ever-burning world, set aflame by none other than him, discomfited him just a touch, for he instinctively knew that flames which were never quenched had a clear *infernal* connotation.

"But what about—"

He spoke these words aloud, naked, on his unmade bunk bed in his trailer, but for some reason he only completed the thought in his mind. The word he silently pronounced was purgatory.

Again, Evan had very little formal acquaintance with theological notions; what he knew, he sensed on a kind of gut level. Somehow or other, he had caught wind of the principle of this realm, where wretched beings went, not to be punished, but rather, to be purified. There, the flames would burn hot and long as well, but though one's trial by fire might last a millennium or an eon, it would not last forever. One day, one wonderful day, it would end, and one would be enabled to enter Paradise. That very surety made one's ordeal bearable.

"Purgatory."

Now he spoke the word aloud, for it brought at least a temporary resolution to the cognitive dissonance which had been troubling him. "I must go on," he whispered. "I must go all the way. I must walk the burning path to my destination. My destination is that very eternally burning conflagration which leaves none untouched, least of all myself... Purgatory...yes, a purge! A purge must happen..."

There came a soft knock at the door, and seconds later, Eveline entered the trailer, closing and locking the door behind her, an exultant expression lighting up her face.

"Evan, oh Evan. You were magnificent, really magnificent tonight." She spoke reverentially, as one speaks to one's guru, rather than to one's son. Moreover, and more peculiarly (so the scene would have struck any bystander, anyway), she was not in the least put off by Evan's nakedness. Nor did Evan make any effort to cover himself.

Instead he almost mechanically stood, and soon they were in one another's arms, she smothering his cheeks with breathy kisses. "Darling, my darling, my sweet, dear one," she purred. "You are a good boy, oh you are the *best, best, best* boy..."

Evan felt himself grow rapidly aroused, as he had on so many previous, similar occasions. Her touch comforted, refreshed, and enthralled him, yet he found some part of his consciousness attempting to resist, even as Eveline disrobed, bared her breasts, pressed her stiffening nipples against him, even as her mouth met his, parted, even as their tongues mingled together.

"Eveline, please," he feebly stammered, between hot, wet kisses.

"Don't call me *that,*" she readily answered, without missing a beat, as if she had expected to hear it all along.

"Agatha, could we please, not now..." he whispered, but with weakening resolve.

"Don't call me that, either," she shot back, grinning as she pulled down her underwear, grabbed his now fully erect organ, and began to caress it.

Evan, sighed, gave up, gave in, as it seemed he always did.

"Mother," he groaned. "Oh mother, mother, mother..."

"Oh, son," she cried out as they fell together onto his bunk and she straddled him and he entered her, "my dear, precious son. My child, my love, my life, my, my...leader!"

With each generous thrust of her hips, she felt, she was enabling him to lead her, giving him the potency needed to take her exactly where she needed to go, where they all needed to go. Suddenly, as if catching her thoughts, he caught her up, flung her onto the bunk, and now he was atop her; now it was his thrusts which were truly leading her, and himself, and all the rest of the world, to sweet, sure, rapturous delight.

"Lead me, leader," she unabashedly exulted. "Lead us all! Take us down the path, take us there!"

Her fingernails dug like beastly talons into her son's back as Eveline flung back her head and glided dreamily into ecstasy.

"Dad! Dad, wake up!"

Julius Ambien could discern the voice of his daughter, but only faintly. Her words were buried beneath what could only be described as an avalanche of terror.

He perceived it merely as terror, yet it was in fact nothing so generic; in truth, it needed some more specific appellation, but none were immediately forthcoming, so "terror" would simply have to do. This terror was inchoate and formless, yet it was loud and shrill; it pulsated with an awful intensity, emitting sounds that resembled the screams of a helpless infant being subjected to inconceivable trauma...

If he could only *reach into* the terror, and bring aid to the distressed child! But he was stuck, immobilized, and prevented from doing anything. He twisted mightily to escape, but something held all of his joints in check. He began to cry out, though words escaped him, seemed alien to him, seemed a mockery to him. He screamed in rage, in grief, in unrestrained vituperation against that very terror which was subjecting that child, *his* child, to such obscene depredations...he wailed helplessly and, managing somehow to break free from the shackles which held him in check, flailed with all of his strength, trying to get at the terror, to beat it back, even though he knew in fact he was no match for it.

And worst of all! It taunted him. For he, in truth, had brought about this set of circumstances...if not for him, this poor child, his child, would not be enduring such torment. Consumed with this devastating knowledge, Julius began to howl with full-throated despair...

"Dad! Dad, wake up! It's just a dream! Wake up!" His daughter's voice, terror-stricken as it was, now seemed pitched into a cacophonous discord with the noises that predominated in his dream...dream! He was dreaming! He became aware that his daughter was shaking him by the arm, desperately attempting to attempt to achieve his awakening. He must wake! But the terror seemed to hold him ever tighter! Would he remain forever in this nightmare?

Suddenly, something wet and cold smacked against his face, and Julius found his eyes shooting open. The first sight that greeted his now awakened gaze was of his daughter, her lovely face contorted with distress, her eyes reddened with tears. She was holding an empty bucket, the contents of which she had evidently just poured over his face to assist him in regaining consciousness.

Seeing that he was awake, she yelled, "Daddy!" and leaped to embrace him. For a minute or so, she rocked him softly back and forth, in a manner patently maternal, as he continued to weep.

"Daddy," he whispered. "You were dreaming again. This is the fifth night in a row...I can't handle seeing you like this..."

Julius inhaled deeply, and seeking to regain his manly pride, willed himself to cease sobbing. It was not real, he told himself. Yet as soon as he attempted to soothe himself with such a sentiment, a foreboding immediately seized him afresh.

It was real. Somehow. But what did it mean, exactly?

Beatrix Ambien— formerly "Unit 1410-B" of the "Lilith Line," who had taken the "B" in her designated title in order to create a proper name for herself— knew better than to trouble her father with questions. She knew already everything there was to know about what was disturbing his sleep. She wished she knew much less than she did, in fact; the knowledge she possessed chafed painfully against her consciousness.

21 years ago they had first met, under circumstances that could only be described as extreme.

She had been twelve at the time, but she little knew anything about age, having been brought up in a manner that was purposefully chaotic. She had, in fact, been frequently reminded of her disposability by that mysterious conglomerate of officials who had "raised" her. She had only been fed and clothed in order that she might eventually be presented as a necessary sacrifice (so she had been informed, in so many words); but along the way, as a supposedly untenable "hybrid"—another principle which she could not initially understand, and which was never really explained to her, but which she eventually took, again, to mean that she was patently disposable, because, being neither fish nor fowl, she served no real purpose in this world.

Nevertheless, her handlers did not neglect her, much as she wished they would, considering the sort of attention they paid her. Neglect, by comparison, would have been a kindness.

Instead, they gave her a great deal of scrutiny, in the process, subjecting her to endless ordeals that strained her endurance to the limit. While (unbeknownst to her) other little girls were going to school, playing with dolls, celebrating birthday parties, and engaging in other happy rituals of childhood, this sad "hybrid" was living a life filled with trauma and largely drained of joy.

The result of the heartless experimentation was not, however, totally absent of fruitfulness. Due in part to the uniqueness of her DNA, and perhaps also due to the manner with which she was regimentally tormented (since systematic abuse often yields results, though they are hardly worth the costs, at least from the oft-unheard perspective of the abused herself), she had developed various talents which very much set her apart. Mostly these involved telekinesis. Her handlers (which is to say, her torturers and jailers), however, always made sure to keep these powers contained; the few times she had dared to use her telekinetic abilities as a means of attempting escape—a notion she grasped as deeply desirable, though she little knew what it looked like, other than it would mean being free from the pain to which she was regularly subjected via various methods, each awful in its own unique way—her handlers would see to it that she was severely punished.

This did not, however, break the spirit of this resilient creature. she simply learned that she needed to bide her time, and surely an opportunity would arise whereby she could manage to find a way out of the prison into which she had been born, and in which she was eventually meant to die.

Of course, it little helped that she had literally no one with whom she could share her daily miseries, and thus was denied of the catharsis afforded by commiseration with another soul. For this reason, she created a being to whom she regularly communicated, but only in her mind, never out loud, and only during such moments when she wasn't aware of being watched or otherwise espied by others. For attention, to her, was never a good thing; thus, unlike most children her age, she never wished for it, much less attempted to attract it.

She did not know exactly what to call this being with whom she communicated during quiet moments, mostly when she was pretending to be asleep. In fact, the notion of giving it a name didn't really occur to her, since in the place where she had been consigned to dwell, no one had proper names. Her chief instructor and handler was a woman whom she had been instructed to refer to as "Mother," but in truth, there was little that could be called motherly about her. All of her handlers were cruel and rapacious to varying degrees, but none of the others possessed the uniquely frightening aspect of Mother.

Mother had, to put it delicately, certain insatiable drives. It was pointless to attempt to divert her from what she wanted when she was in one of her "moods," which unfortunately, was often. And doubly unfortunate was the fact that this "hybrid," being the only one of her kind, was of especial interest to Mother. Whilst enduring such depredations, our "hybrid" spoke secretly to the being she had created (or had she rather *discovered* this entity?), and it spoke back in mournful tones, indicating an awareness of and sympathy for her wretched and humiliated state of suffering.

At first, these ordeals left her sobbing pitifully. Then she came to realize that her upset feelings only excited Mother and caused her horrifically fevered desires to grow all the more ardent. Finally, however, and with a great relief, she found herself floating towards that glorious state beyond the pain, the place of *disassociation.* When she managed to drift away to this spot, nothing could hurt her; her entire frame became charged with a numbed aura of sheer bliss.

It was at these moments when her inner friend spoke to her most tenderly, in a manner that no person had ever addressed her before. The friend's voice assured her that she was not a mistake, that she had been born for a purpose, that she was valuable, and that she was loved. The friend's voice didn't so much *say* these notions verbatim as it did whisper these ideas through some indeterminate aperture of her apprehension. Nevertheless, she "heard" them, and took them to heart, though she made sure never to betray her heart's response to the reception of such encouraging words. She felt like weeping for the joy of knowing that someone or something outside of herself-- outside of her hostile, cruel, and unforgiving environment-- cared for her, treasured her even, in some form or fashion that she didn't exactly understand but was no less real for all of that. However, she knew better than to weep in front of Mother, or in front of any of the rest of her handlers, or even in front of the "Liliths," that is to say, the line of clones that surrounded her every day, who were subjected to many of the same outrages and abuses as she, but who, she was given to understand, were not a "hybrid" like herself.

This hybrid, in fact, had been given to understand that one of these beautiful clones had in fact given birth to her, in a process that humans call a "pregnancy." Very little else was revealed to her, except that this event defied what most in her cohort understood to be "possible," as the Lilliths were believed to be sterile, meaning incapable of becoming pregnant... so, why had it happened with her? And who, among all of the clones of the Lilith line, had managed the feat of birthing her, and *how,* and *why?* When she asked these questions, she was told that they were unimportant, and that she should just forget them, and furthermore warned that *if she persisted in wondering these things, the outcome would be very bad for her.* She had been around long enough to know what that meant; it didn't even register to her nascent mind as a threat, per se, simply a consequence of remaining in a headspace that was meant to remain unoccupied.

Little did she know that her handlers had told her these things in order to run a kind of experiment on her: they wished to see how knowledge of such matters would impact her behavior and personality. To them, she was a living, breathing science experiment. Telling her the truth about certain aspects of her existence was considered advantageous in the sense that it would enhance her overall discombobulation; her handlers had decided a while ago that keeping her perpetually off-balance would be most desirable. They were thus even more cruel to her than they were to the Liliths, or at least more arbitrary in the cruelty they applied. The Lilith units, after all, served a definable purpose for the organization; they existed to further their goals of continued domination over world leaders via spycraft, seduction, and blackmail. But she, the "hybrid," being neither fish nor fowl (and in truth knowing little about either), was a sort of wildcard. She possessed no known utility, except as a subject of curiosity.

When you are a subject of curiosity, and those whose curiosity you arouse have endlessly sophisticated manners of poking and prodding you, and a concomitant absence of what "common" people commonly call "conscience," then one is faced with a frightening and treacherous path. But she, the hybrid, felt strengthened to walk that path, because of the encouragement provided by her inner friend, who spoke to her with such tenderness that she couldn't help but weep with joy; of course, as previously stated, she only gave vent to such sentiments when she knew no one else was about-- namely, as she lay in her bed at night.

They had provided her with a private room, whereas the Lilith units all slept in bunks. The Liliths, after all, were naught but a collective, although some units fared better than others, and those who proved ineffective were simply discontinued, while those who showed a greater proclivity to excel at their tasks were, in a sense, "promoted." But they nevertheless tended to be seen as generally interchangeable with one another, whilst she, the hybrid, stood apart.

It should go without saying, by the way, that they never named her. They even called her "It," as if she were unworthy of being granted a personal pronoun. But her inner friend told her that she was indeed a girl, and that she possessed a name, even if no one had chosen to bestow her with the dignity requisite to give her a name, this did not mean that she was not in fact, a named person, even if she did not yet know what her name was.

"You will find out soon," her inner voice assured her.

"But, what must happen, first?" she asked the voice. Upon putting this question to her invisible friend, she felt sure for a moment that she sensed that the being, with whom she conversed, had endured a spasm of grief. Finally, it replied, "You will be tested, terribly tested. You will undergo a trial unlike any you have previously known. But you must be strong. If you are strong, you will be delivered from that which brings you pain and terror."

"Who will be my deliverer?" she asked.

"He will initially be brought in, a victim like yourself. He will be used for purposes which elude his understanding. But he will come to his senses and break the chains of your bondage. He will not touch you in the foul way that these people, both men and women, do. He will love and care for you after the manner of a proper father."

"A *father?*" she repeated. She had heard that word before, a few times, but had never understood what it was meant to signify. The times the word had been spoken around her, it had always been in an offhand way. One of the staff would mention his or her "dad." "If my dad knew what I was doing, he would have a heart attack!" was one such statement which emerged. As a "heart attack" was clearly, contextually speaking, a reaction of extreme shock, stemming from apparent disapproval, she figured at first that fathers, or "dads," were just the sort of people who got easily shocked, and who perhaps disapproved of what was going on in such a place as where she and the Liliths were kept. If so, then a father must be one who could be trusted, since what went on in the dwelling place she shared with her tormentors was undeniably grotesque, abusive, and awful.

Yet for all that, the daily abuse that she endured at the hands of Mother and her minions was pretty much all that she knew. She could scarcely fathom anything different, and yet, she perceived, somehow, that things could be different, even if she could not easily envisage this alternative manner of living, in which abuse and misery were absent.

In her dreams, where her wonderful, always unseen friend spoke to her, she thought that she gained an inkling of what it would mean not to live in Hell. Again, she didn't use the word "Hell," because the concept was utterly foreign to her, yet if she were somehow able to relate her day-to-day experiences to a sympathetic listener, there is little doubt that the latter would characterize her environment in just such a manner. However, her unseen friend didn't dwell on such matters (why tell her what she already knew?), but rather encouraged her to be vigilant, to wait for the coming of the man who would free her, the one who would prove himself worthy to be her father.

"And your mother, too, your true mother, loves you very much," her voice told her.

These words were a wondrous balm to her troubled heart, though they carried a certain mystery. How could anyone, other than the horrible woman she knew as "Mother," be her Mother? What did that even mean?

One day, Mother—that is, the foul being whom she had always known as "Mother"—called upon Unit 1410-B.. This was never a good sign, but by now she knew to put on a brave face; it came naturally to one who had endured the litany of tribulations which had plagued her since infancy, if not before. Had she known the word "disassociation" and its meaning, she would have readily grasped it with a patently native acuity. As it was, she knew the experience of it without even having a name to give to it. In fact, she comprehended little in the way of actual language at this point. Mostly she grasped things in a precognitive, pre-verbal manner; like a feral animal, she possessed a patently primal sense of the world that surrounded her. Instinctively, she knew when to keep her head down; inwardly, she knew when to escape into her mind to block out that which would harm her if she focused upon it or even paid attention to it in any way.

When she entered Mother's office, she saw that accompanying her was a man, one whom she had never before seen. He was portly and squat, and his eyes were shrewd. He looked her over as if inspecting luggage, then turned to Mother and said, "This is the *miracle?* What's so *miraculous* about her?"

His cynical tone was met by a tut-tutting rebuke from Mother.

"Darling," she said, "You must learn to look beneath the surface. True, she appears rather unremarkable. She lacks the beauty of our Liliths, and within her there is no evidence of what makes them worthwhile to us as assets, namely, their seductive cunning. But Unit 1410-B here nevertheless retains a quality that they all lack, a quality that makes her unique and valuable."

The man grabbed my face roughly and stared into my eyes with an intense gaze, as if attempting to locate that elusive "quality" that was deemed to be of value. Then he pushed my face away.

"I don't see it, Eveline," he pronounced, before his lips twisted into a crooked smile. "Of course, I cannot lie. She looks like she'd be fun for a few minutes. You know my type, don't you, darling?"

Mother (whose name was also Eveline, apparently) responded with a playful smack at the man's arm. "You dirty old bastard," she responded with a lilting giggle, which was a bit startling to hear since Mother/Eveline had never displayed any sort of girlish affectation before, at least not in her presence.

The man began to favor me with a lecherous smirk, and started to stroke my chest. "Ahhh, mere buds. Still developing. So very nice..." As he groped me, I found myself suddenly struck with revulsion, which caught me off guard, since I had been violated in many different ways and by now tended simply to disassociate when I sensed that such an unpleasant interaction was about to begin. But now, that voice was whispering to me that I in fact had the power to destroy this fat, leering creep if I wanted to do so. I managed to keep my wits about me and hid my true feelings behind the blank stare I always assumed when in a determinedly dissociative state. But presently, I became aware that Mother had slapped his hand away and he had withdrawn it from intimate contact with my bosom with a look of annoyance.

"You stupid *cunt—*" he began.

"Eye on the prize, Evan!" she rebuked him, unfazed by his demeanor or his insults. "You can't always think with your lower half. We have to preserve her for the sacrifice."

The fat man's face registered shock. "You mean..."

"Yes, Evan. She is the one. She is the miracle which we must feed to the beastmaker."

At this point, Evan's expression changed entirely. He also began to look at me differently, with an odd sort of reverence suddenly replacing the lust which had formerly animated his being.

"She is the offspring of a Lilith and a man. She should not exist. Her being here is an impossibility. Liliths do not menstruate. They do not produce eggs. So how was our girl here formed in the womb of a Lilith?

The man, Evan Crumple, shook his head with wonder. "I'm not sure I like this."

"What do you mean?" snapped Mother.

Evan just seemed caught up by the sheer uncanniness of it all. He said nothing. Mother thus changed the subject. "Have you taken in the 'man of wrath?'"

"Yes," Evan answered. "He is a believer. He has joined my campaign staff. He little knows what is happening to him. We have taken him up and brought him along on our ride."

"Perfect," Mother purred. "Our Liliths are remarkable. No man is any match for their charms."

"It's *your* charms that will have to manage this one," Evan said.

"Oh, don't worry about that. I'm up to the challenge," Mother replied, with an enthusiasm which struck Bea as somehow ghastly, though she little understood the context or what was meant by this reference to Mother's alleged 'charms.'

"But this one," Evan said, eyeing her again. "What role is she meant to play?"

"She is a miracle! Half-Lilith, half-man… She is the only one of her kind!"

Evan continued to study Bea as one would scrutinize some enigmatic object whose ultimate purpose was maddeningly elusive. Sensing the man's lack of comprehension, Mother suddenly seized Evan's face, in much the same manner that he had seized hers moments earlier. With peculiar emphasis, she spelled it out for him:

"*Think* of the potency she represents as a sacrifice!"

Hearing these words, his eyes lit up in a manner which once again struck her as ghastly, as offputting as her enthusiasm for using her "charms" had been, if not more so.

One night, there was widespread jubilation amongst the staff who ran the facility where she spent most of her time. What had happened? She heard only snatches of conversation:

"Crumple won the Senate race. He's in!"

"Knew it would happen."

"Crumple and Mother are gonna take things to the next level for us! Finally, all of our work will pay off…"

What she experienced next was a whirligig of sights, sounds, and sensations. It was the occasion of what was being called the "harvest," but she had little clue what that meant, although she suspected the worst. Still, the voice within quietly whispered to be attuned to her environment; she was most assuredly in danger, it told her, but even as danger drew close, her rescue was all the more imminent. "The darkness will yield to the dawn," was a phrase that resounded in her soul, and continued to resound, even as she became aware that her captors were holding her down, injecting her in the arm with some substance that caused her to feel sleepy…

What followed were mostly impressions: they moved her body to a car, which drove for some distance. She had seldom been out of the facility before, and something within her stirred at this new experience, yet the drugs they had forced into her system made everything seem more like a dream, or like a series of events she was witnessing rather than participating in; it was real, yet it seemed more like a flight of fancy… Yet there was an increasingly ominous force, something anything but fanciful, which seemed to bear down upon her the closer they drew to their mysterious destination…

Hands lifting her out of the car, which apparently had previously come to a stop, though her mind hadn't registered that occurrence. Hands taking her into a house, out in the countryside. Men guarding the door making deferential little grunts, stepping away, allowing them egress. Then: more grunts and groans, a cacophony of such sounds, like numerous couples in the act of coupling, all to some pervasive, ritualistic rhythm…then down a flight of stairs into a musty, close, cramped room. She is placed down on the floor, which isn't a floor at all; it is mere dirt. She is unclothed. Has she always been such, from the beginning of the night? Consciousness starting to return. Wanting it to dissolve again into dreaminess, trying to will herself back to that prior state of drowse, but to no avail.

Then: the presence of Mother, Evan, and a Lilith…and someone else. Another man. The man and Lilith and Mother groan and grunt together; they are all naked, too. The new man seems to be in the same state as her, floating in and out of focus, aware and unaware at once. He is in pleasure and in distress simultaneously, unsure where one sensation ends and the other begins. She becomes slowly tuned in to something new: pain. Pain, excruciating pain, between her legs, the familiar place. Evan had hurt her there; had she even screamed? The screams were coming back to her, reaching her from the very recent past. They echoed in her ears; why had she not heard them when she was screaming, why had she not felt the pain between her legs when it was being inflicted by Evan? Had it been mere standard disassociation on her part, or the drugs they had given her, or both?

Now Evan, repulsively nude, was pushing this new man towards her, encouraging him to complete what he had begun, so he could finally assume the place amongst the firmament of grandeur, or some such; perhaps Beatrix had been hallucinating those words; perhaps this entire ordeal was only happening in her head, but even so, she could not deny that it was indeed real, much as she would prefer things to be otherwise. The man in question, bleary-eyed and haggard, regarded her wounded form with wonder and pity; instantly Beatrix knew that he was the one, the man with the bleary eyes would not hurt her.

His hesitation in the face of a clear command enraged Evan, who declared he would perform the needful task himself; he pushed the man out of the way and set upon her with rough and all-too-familiar hands, and began to violate her anew. She heard her own whimpering voice pleading that he spare her, but by that moment she had already mentally disengaged into the familiar dissociative state. Vaguely, as if from a great distance, she grew conscious that the man had grabbed Evan up off of her and was now beating him with remorseless abandon, before finally snapping his neck. Then the Lilith flung herself at him, screaming, biting his ear, hissing that he had no dominion here, and that "the child is ours, to do with as we please!" The man pulled this vicious monster off his back and pummeled her with a similarly relentless assault, striking her continuously with his fists until her face was completely gone... In her disassociated state, Beatrix registered such a horrifying event with mere curiosity, rather than alarm.

Then words were passed between the man and Mother, upon whom the man clearly intended to unleash his vengeance. Yet even as he set upon her with his murderous rage, she managed to tell him something which caused him to pause, and to stagger back, regarding her with wonder and incredulity. Then he punched the wall next to her, causing her to flinch, before he raised his finger and gave her some kind of severely-worded warning. Presently he left her side, picked Beatrix up with surprising tenderness and care (given the fact that those hands now holding her had done such frightful damage to the flesh and bone of those who sought to harm her mere moments earlier)...

It was through the intervention of this man, Julius Ambien, that Beatrix had escaped from certain death, and broken free from her captors. The next day, she met the man, a doctor, no less, who had been her technical "father," a man who all along had thought she had been aborted, and who was not at all happy to see her, or Julius, alive. In fact, he tried to kill them both, before Beatrix found herself intervening, causing the man to turn the weapon on himself and fire a bullet into his own brain. It marked the first time that she had used her Lilith-derived telekinetic powers, and though it had indeed been unfortunate to kill the man whose seed had miraculously fertilized the womb of her mother, Beatrix knew at the time that her real father had been the man who had rescued her from her depraved network of abusers, so whatever she could do to protect him (as well as herself) was an absolute necessity.

Still, the effect of being on the giving, rather than the receiving end, of pain, torment, and terror—for the unfortunate doctor, it must have felt terrible indeed to find oneself involuntarily turning one's gun on oneself, not to mention involuntarily pulling the trigger—had a strange effect on Beatrix. Though she tried to keep this from herself, and from Julius, the man whom she would in time come to know as her "Dad," she in fact rather *enjoyed* the sensation of being simultaneous judge, jury, and executioner, especially when it came to people she knew had contributed, whether directly or indirectly, to her own subjugation and misery.

Beatrix never spoke openly about how murdering her actual father, albeit in self-defense, caused her to feel a triumphant elation so intense that it frightened her. She wasn't sure what her "voice," that inner entity who had assisted her through her years filled with daily trauma, would think of this development. That voice, in fact, had begun to make itself scarce as soon as she was liberated; she was left on her own, for the most part. The message seemed to be, *I got you to where you ardently desired to go. I delivered you from the hands of your tormenters into the hands of your deliverer. From henceforth, it's up to you. For the duration of the time you are given, you must deliver yourself.*

Now, seeing her father, or the man she had come to know as "Dad," thrashing about in agony for the third night in a row, Beatrix found herself again in the unaccustomed role of witness to the severe distress and trauma of another, that "other" being the very man who had rescued her from Hell, who had remained such a stolid figure in her life for the past two decades.

During those 20 years, the two of them had dwelt together and determinedly survived, even as the society around them suffered its horrific, terminal spiral.

Julius was officially dead, and Beatrix had never officially existed, so both of them were afforded cover of a kind, after a fashion. Run-of-the-mill local constabularies could hardly bother to expend much effort on such as them, provided that they kept their heads down. Every effort was thus made to "go gray," to dress and behave in a manner that succeeded in preventing the attraction of attention.

Local cops were one thing, but higher-level agencies were another matter entirely. Julius knew that such as these had no doubt been dispatched in order to "close the loop" with regard to his and Beatrix's inconvenient existences. Cameras, drones, and surveillance devices were everywhere, though there were far fewer of such devices the more one drifted from the megacities, which was where more and more of the population was settling, as that was where most of the jobs were.

Rural regions, increasingly deserted in accord with the "green" policies of the appointed social planners, made a far easier place to remain inconspicuous. Thus Julius and Beatrix spent most of their time in these vast sectors of largely depopulated wilderness.

Neither of them had had much experience living off the land, so they had to learn on the go. What choice, after all, did they have? They managed to learn to forage and to hunt, and to construct makeshift shelters out of bark, pine needles, and whatever else presented itself as available.

Through the first few years, they managed mainly to avoid human contact. They never stayed in one place for too long, and always conscientiously covered their tracks. Occasionally, they ran across the odd small town in which at least some of the population remained, having refused to be herded to the megacities. Such hardscrabble folk tended to be suspicious of outsiders, but one sight of Julius and Beatrix tended to lower the defenses of even the most cantankerous of outliers and bitter-enders. There was clearly no ounce of guile in this pair. The trauma each had suffered could easily be discerned in their thin, wan, unsmiling faces.

For obvious reasons, the Beatrix's blossoming beauty could at times become a flashpoint, both for the best as well as the very worst of reasons. The sight of a young woman—as Beatrix was certainly becoming—with a clearly tragic backstory, has functioned as a Muse for many a human soul with artistic and empathic proclivities. And in such desperate times as these, the very sight of this girl, her very existence a miracle (though of course none except Julius knew of the exact details pertaining to this miracle), drove many an observer to inspiration and renewed hope.

On the other hand, the girl's striking looks brought the wrong kind of attention from those of a lecherous orientation. Several of these sorts would shamelessly shamble up to Julius and inquire about a transaction, in which they would be granted a block of time alone with Beatrix. Julius, fighting back the gorge that rose within his breast every time he was forced to field such inquiries, and remembering how important it was to remain "gray," would reply tersely that the girl wasn't for sale.

Not that there was truly anything to fear, considering Beatrix's secret abilities. If it ever became necessary, but only as a last resort, she was perfectly able to defend herself.

Eventually, Julius and Beatrix stumbled across a tiny community which warmed to them, where they opted to remain for a while. The town essentially consisted of a desultory row of rusted out campers and trailers planted on a hillside next to a muddy lake (hence its appellation, "Lakeside"); the town's de facto matriarch, a petite, middle-aged redhead that everyone called "Mayor," seemed particularly drawn to the pair. She told them that they could stay in one of the recently vacated places ("Folks tend to come and go a lot around here," she muttered sadly, as a sort of explanation of the availability of the unit); they could stay as long as they liked, provided each of them "pulled their weight," either in tending the crops, which were planted in an adjoining field, or managing the nearby barnyard, with its chickens and pigs, or hunting, or fishing.

The "Mayor" had won her title, it turned out, due to the fact that, in the years leading up to the series of catastrophes that led to the decimation of much of the rural population, she had won that title in a town called Little Hope. The Mayor—whose actual name was Deborah, as she somewhat shyly revealed to Julius a few days after their arrival—had enjoyed her duties as political leader of the town so much that she felt she neglected her marriage. She now bitterly regretted how she had driven her husband away, but she felt even worse that she had alienated her son.

"I felt myself to be the mother of the whole town," Deborah admitted. "There was so much work to be done that I spent less and less time at home. Eventually Thomas (her increasingly estranged husband) told her that he was leaving her for another woman in a different town; he served her divorce papers, and promptly left. Not long after that, their son was drafted to the military to be shipped to Taiwan, which had just been invaded by the Chinese army.

"He was happy to go," Deborah recalled with grave forlornity. "My son, my own flesh, my own blood...he was done with me, just like Thomas was. I lost everything, my whole family. My husband, then my son. They were gone. It was like a mighty one-two punch from God..."

Deborah related these details to Julius and Beatrix like one might speak to a priest in a Confessional booth; though her voice quavered frequently, she seemed most interested in putting forth the hard facts. Beatrix listened somewhat coolly, unsure of how to feel about what she was hearing. Julius, however, found himself intrigued, if not enraptured by Deborah's account of her life. They three of them sat together in what the folks of Lakeside jocularly called the "Mayor's Palace," which was in fact a sparsely-furnished trailer, filled with very few effects. One picture dominated the tiny dresser which adjoined the little twin bed, that of a smiling young man dressed in what looked like tragically incongruous army fatigues; the incongruity of the attire stemmed from the fact that the boy looked far too young to be wearing them. They almost seemed like a Halloween costume, given the lad's boyish features.

Seeing the boy had an unexpected effect on Julius, though he did his best to contain the strange grief that it caused him to experience. He asked if Deborah had heard from her boy at all, and if she knew his whereabouts.

"He hasn't written me once," she stated flatly, adding, with a stifled sob, "I can't say as I blame him at all...I just wish he could forgive me...in trying to be the mother of the entirety of Little Hope, I neglected to be a mother to my son..."

The town had officially been closed down by federal authorities a year ago, in accord with new environmental regulations. Little Hope had come to an end, as had so many other small towns across the country, because the planners in DC had decided that it was time to begin the next phase of their "Reset," which, under cover of preservationist rhetoric, in fact sought to enforce the resettlement of much of the rural population to the megacity regions.

Thus had commenced what many called the "Trail of Tears 2.0," in which hundreds of thousands, then millions of people had desultorily trekked from their hometowns, where many of their families had dwelt for generations, to be herded, first into camps, then into "tiny home" tenement blocks in blighted communities on the outskirts of metropolitan areas. The death toll accrued by this forced resettlement project was mostly unknown, since no official source was keeping count (and those who offered estimates were predictably charged with the crime of "promoting misinformation," now a felonious offense in many states), but stories abounded of numerous suicides, as well as not a few outbreaks of disease in the camps, which were woefully understaffed and inefficient at providing sustenance or administering medical care.

Those few who refused to be obedient to the directive to desert the rural regions were, in many cases, tracked down, arrested, and shipped to detainee centers for an indeterminate period of time. It was rumored—though few put such accounts down on official channels on the internet or elsewhere, for fear of the aforementioned rash of "anti-misinformation" legislation, which made challenging the prevailing corporate-governmental party line a serious crime—that such miscreants were often dispatched via firing squad and buried in unmarked mass graves. Still, these fearful whispers generated enough fear in people's hearts that they were, more often than not, persuaded to comply with authoritative decrees—however dubious their lawfulness, in a Constitutional sense—sent down from on high.

Once they reached the cities, many a young man, and even a few young women, received an abrupt summons to serve in one of several ongoing wars that were currently afoot. Some found themselves bound for Iran, where ground war fighting had grown especially fierce; others were shipped to Eastern Europe, where the disputed Balkan territories were ever shifting between NATO-backed troops on one side and Russian and Chinese forces on the other; others, finally—indeed the bulk of the new recruits—were dispatched to the straits of Taiwan, which was locked in a grim proxy war with invaders from the Mainland. But other youngsters, like Deborah's dear son Thomas, actually didn't wait to get drafted, instead volunteering to leave his mother and father behind out of seemingly youthful spite. For Thomas, Deborah sadly told us, the resettlement campaign had provided the perfect opportunity to opt out entirely.

"I hope, I pray to see him again," she pronounced with determination. "Once this insanity finally ceases."

"Will that ever happen?" asked Beatrix. It was the first time she had spoken.

Deborah cast her a look, her face unexpectedly hardened. "It will end, sooner than anyone thinks."

Taken aback as he was by this answer, Julius found himself even more surprised by how Beatrix responded with stony-faced silence, almost as if she were distracted by some distressing intrusive thought.

When he asked her about it later, Beatrix just shrugged, declining to elaborate or even comment on her unspoken response. Julius knew better than to push his young companion on the matter; like every prudent father, he knew better than to attempt to force his stubborn, willful adopted daughter to admit more than she wished to.

Julius, however, found himself increasingly drawn to conversing with the "Mayor." Something within him wished to open up to her, yet something else within him, equally insistent, opted to hold himself in check. So he settled merely for spending time in her presence, in conversations increasingly held in Beatrix's absence.

There was something oddly comforting about dwelling with her, which he couldn't quite describe. Her face, though weathered by loss, stress, and hardship, still retained a vitality that manifested occasionally in ways that seemed practically wondrous. Sometimes she would smile through her tears in a way that seemed not merely defiant, but triumphant. Julius saw at those moments that she wasn't merely refusing to succumb to despair, but that she had in some sense already leapt through the present darkness; her soul was now bathing in some eternal light.

Was she an angel? He found himself asking himself that question several times, before deploring himself for entertaining such an embarrassing fantasy. Yet he could not escape the suspicion that something in her general demeanor seemed to belong to some more exalted plane. How had she found her way there? How had she managed to return to this troubled world, still somehow carrying that celestial aura with her? It was a secret he longed to uncover.

Meanwhile, of course, both Julius and Beatrix conscientiously did their parts to keep the collective supplied with sustenance. Bea tended the garden (it had been discovered some time ago that she possessed that proverbial "green thumb," though of course she had never had even the slightest acquaintance with the term). Julius, once quite squeamish about the notion of doing harm to living things, now found hunting to be an entirely agreeable enterprise. He loved handling a rifle (such weapons, which had largely been confiscated when the "Trail of Tears" was enforced, were still abundant amongst the so-called "bitter-enders" who had hung back, hidden themselves, and still lived illegally in the heartland). It gave him a sense of peace to stalk through the forest, his .308 Winchester slung over his shoulder, to stake out a position and then wait in utter stillness for the faint sound of hoof tracks across the fallen leaves and foliage.

When his shots met their intended target, and the beast stumbled and fell, Julius did not feel that he had transgressed any moral laws. He did not even feel like a killer. Instead, it was as though he were simply participating in nature's intimate processes. This beast he had felled was a necessary sacrifice. He returned to the encampment that evening, and many nights afterwards, with a swell of pride in his chest, a feeling to which he was unaccustomed.

Deborah always found time to greet him upon his return, and to praise him for the carcass which he carried into town in his hunter's pack. Julius took these greetings in stride, with a stoic countenance, but could hardly deny the thrill which her approving glances and words of encouragement gave him.

One particular evening in late autumn, when a chill had overtaken the air and the first frosts were accumulating on the grass and in the trees, Julius found himself in the Mayor's trailer, with one of her blankets wrapped around his midsection to stave off the cold, as she stoked the embers in the unit's makeshift fireplace. He had informed Bea that he had been invited to dine with Deborah, and she had received this news perfunctorily, with a nod. She had been invited too, but she demurred, declaring that she was tired. Julius was overtaken with a pang of guilt when he realized that he was happy to hear that she had declined to attend, as he much preferred to be alone with Deborah. Could Beatrix tell? Was she inwardly sulking at the amount of attention that the Mayor had won from him recently?

With Bea, again, he knew better than to attempt to pry answers. Instead, he made an effort, sincere but half-hearted, to insure her that he continued to love her desperately and care deeply for her well-being, and to add that he hoped she was enjoying this sort-of respite from "roughing it" that had been experiencing since stumbling upon Lakeside quite by accident. "I mean, we are still 'roughing it,' but it's a lot nicer to have a roof over our heads and to be part of a community rather than wandering forest nomads, right?" he asked, making an effort at levity. She smiled faintly, indicating that she appreciated his gesture, even if she didn't exactly feel inclined to be more openly communicative at present.

"She's been through a lot. A hell of a lot," Julius told Deborah. They had finished their meal of roast venison, garnished with tomatoes and spinach from the garden, and now they were sipping on some of the Mayor's homemade mead.

"I can tell that she loves you deeply," Deborah said. "But girls her age are often hard to handle, even under the best of circumstances."

Julius inquired what Deborah had been like as a teenager, and the latter chuckled ruefully. "A holy terror," she told him. "No scratch that: I was an unholy terror."

She asked about him. "A good man will often neglect his own well-being, thinking that he has no time for such trivialities, but this is a pitfall that he must transcend," she told him. "It is important, from time to time, to treat yourself, and to take advantage of opportunities to lighten your load."

There was so much that he wished to tell her. He sat there, imagining himself relating the events of his whole life. What had pushed him astray after many a year on the straight and narrow. That which had finally shoved him beyond the bounds of being able to tolerate his own existence. Then: the all-consuming desire to die, due to having developed a positive hatred towards life, and by extension, God. How he had become that "man of rage," who had thereafter been used for intolerable ends, to reproduce against his will...

He had closed his eyes, and now snapped them open at a sudden sensation; it was Deborah, who had reached out her hand and was tenderly stroking his cheek. Had he spoken his thoughts out loud, without awareness of having done so?

"You have a son?" she asked, her emerald eyes fixating upon him with great intensity.

Julius started. Had he even said that? She did not seem to notice his bafflement and alarm, but simply continued to let her fingers linger upon his cheek, and then her hand was cupping his jaw.

"You have a son," she repeated, only this time it wasn't a question. "Tell me about him."

I...don't know him. I have never met him.

"How did he come into being? Who is his mother?"

How could he possibly answer that question? He stammered and stuttered, but no words emerged from his mouth.

"How old is he?" she asked, continuing her barrage of questions, all of them asked in the same calm, compassionate tone.

"I don't know," Julius answered, almost in a whisper. It had been some time since he had even thought about this matter. It had always lingered in the back of his mind, but he seldom permitted it entrance into his consciousness. For the last several years, there had been plenty to occupy his attention in an immediate sense, and little time for contemplation.

She finally moved her hand away from his face and leaned back in her chair. “We have that in common. A son, a missing son.”

Julius nodded, grateful that, at the very least, the seeming inquisition had come to an end. Deborah drained the rest of her mead, set it on the table, and declared a sort of denouement:

“I have a feeling that we will be of great help to one another.”

It was that night, upon returning to his and Beatrix's unit, that, upon falling asleep, Julius had his first dream of his son. Or rather, he dreamed about his son.

That is, while his son was the subject of his dream, he never actually saw him. He never even heard his voice. He just saw, as from the perspective of a voyeur, a host of scenes, which shifted in an ominous procession before his eyes. Somehow, he was given to understand, his boy had dwelt in these places. There was a plush and ornate bedroom, furnished with silks and other fine fabrics. A bed in which his child had slept. A hallway, expensively decorated with open windows and curtains swaying in a gentle breeze. He had walked there, inhaling as he did the nearby scent of the sea. Yet all of these images of luxury, comfort, and ease were permeated with a peculair intimation of dread.

His son's presence consistently eluded him, as if he had just departed. Where had he gone? What was he doing? What was being done to him? The last question struck Julius with the force of a hammer's blow, and he woke with a gasp.

"Dad, what's wrong?"

Beatrix's frantic voice assailed his ears and he shook himself.

"You were making strange noises. Groaning and crying." Bathed in the first light of the morning, her face displayed concern mingled with incomprehension.

"Bad dream," he muttered. "Sorry to wake you, Bea."

But the nightmares persisted for the next several nights, culminating in the event on the fifth evening, when he found himself unable to rouse itself, even after gaining awareness that he was indeed dreaming.

When Bea doused him with a bucket of water, it snapped him back to consciousness, yet even after he woke, he was unable to shake the apprehension which had gripped him in his sleep.

Why were these dreams suddenly seizing him with such violence? Why, even when he recalled few if any details, had these nightly visitations begun to take such a toll on his waking life?

The next day, he set out to hunt, like he had on so many previous occasions. This time, however, when he glimpsed his prey through the scope of his rifle, he froze, unable to pull the trigger. For the briefest of moments, he was seized with terror as the head of the deer seemed to assume the face of a man. Or rather, a boy. His features, only momentarily apparent, were unlike any he had ever seen before, yet at the same time hauntingly familiar. He gave a start, and the buck, sensing the disturbance, bounded away deeper into the forest.

Julius collapsed to his knees. Tears stung his eyes. He suddenly hated himself with enough fervor to rip out his own eyeballs. How could he have even contemplated the notion of slaughtering this beautiful beast? And all the times before...all of the murderous violence he had perpetrated upon these creatures on prior occasions. *What was he doing? What had he done?* Another wave of intense self-loathing washed over him and he felt himself returned to his prior desperate state years prior, when he had ardently sought suicide, but never to any avail. The old urge returned with a vengeance, and without even thinking about what he was doing, he turned the rifle's muzzle to the inside of his mouth.

Just before he pulled the trigger, however, some equally ardent impulse or intimation knocked him backwards, and the muzzle flung from his lips, the bullet just grazing his temple as he fell into the snow.

The blast was literally deafening. At least for a long moment. That is to say, Julius, flat on his back, actually heard nothing for an interval. Then, a ringing, so piercing it seemed to rend his head in twain, permeated his entire being. But carried on this ringing was something even more discomfiting. To Julius, it seemed that this ringing transformed into a more terrible noise, namely what sounded very much like the scream of a boy in pain.

That evening, he was telling Deborah about his harrowing encounter with the buck, and all of the things that he thought he saw and heard. When he finished recounting the events, he looked up, shaken, his voice cracking with grief, he found to his consternation that Deborah was smiling.

Incredulous and bewildered, Julius found himself unable to speak. To his further shock, he found that she was reaching out and touching his face, with an expression that could almost be interpreted as playfully pitying.

"Do you *truly* not know yet?" she asked. "Are you *really* still unaware?"

Julius sat silently, let her take both of his hands in hers, so taken aback that he could not fathom what was coming next.

"How about *now?*" she asked, and to Julius's shock, her voice registered as totally different. But what was this new voice, and why did it sound familiar?

Then, before his eyes, he saw her features transform. Her red hair darkened, her eyes turned brighter, her face widened slightly, her nose became more aqualine; even her body grew slightly in stature. Deborah, or the "Mayor," was no longer present. (Had she ever really been present?) In her place was...

"It's you," muttered Julius, entranced quite in spite of himself. Before him, in resplendent glamour, was the woman he had known as Eveline Crumple.

"Oh, *fuckboy,*" purred the woman now standing before him. "My fuckboy. The man of rage himself. You should see our child, your child. Oh, he is a beautiful, beautiful boy. And he is going to change the world.

He wouldn't be here, if not for you..."

Somehow her clothes had melted away. A powerful musk emanated from her pores; it was positively intoxicating, and though he tried his best to resist, he swooned, and his body was immediately charged with desire. She kissed him full on the mouth, then whispered, "Wanna make another baby? Your boy is lonely..." She touched his crotch, felt him stiffen. Julius, entranced, had forgotten himself thoroughly. His surroundings seemed to dissolve around him, so completely was he consumed with the form of the woman who now held him entwined, her bare arms and legs wrapping around him the same way a spider's appendages might encompass the frame of its prey.

Julius could barely see or hear anything at that moment, so consumed was he with the woman who now lay naked on top of him, that he only faintly heard the door to the Deborah's unit swing open.

"Let my father go, you bitch!" screamed a familiar voice, and for a moment the attention of the entity who held him was distracted. He heard an inhuman hiss emerge from her lips, the same lips that had been ardently kissing him seconds earlier.

"You *abomination!"* the creature shrieked. "You monstrous... *halfbreed!"*

"You are not my mother!" Beatrix rejoined. Then the she-beast, still naked, left Julius behind and galloped furiously toward the girl, who apparently stood in the doorway. Julius heard a shot fired, which seemed to miss its mark (had the she-beast, with preternatural dexterity, dodged the bullet that should have felled her)? Then he heard his daughter scream, and leapt up in terror to see that the Eveline-Mother beast had seized Beatrix, yanked the rifle from her grasp, and now had a hand around her neck.

The helpless look upon his daughter's face and the choking sounds emanated from her lips awakened Julius, and launched him into a frenzy. *"Bea!"* he yelled, and leaped at the naked being who had gripped him, who now seemed on the verge of strangling his precious child. Somehow, he managed to wrest the she-beast away momentarily, but her hideous strength kicked in and she flung him away like a ragdoll and charged anew at Beatrix.

Then, in his dazed bewilderment, lying there on the floor smarting from the blow he'd just endured, Julius heard something that confused him still further. Another woman's voice bellowed a lusty yell, and another gunshot rang out, followed by a scream, this time emanating from the she-beast, who now was apparently beating a retreat.

"Run, Mother! Run, but you can't hide!" yelled this new voice. Straining his eyes to see, Julius recognized to his shock the familiar form of...a Lilith!

This Lilith was more aged than the one who had appeared before him so many years ago, a prolonged Muze-induced hallucination nevertheless identical in appearance with the rest of the Lilith cloning line. This older, but still astonishingly beautiful Lilith strode over to Bea, wrapped an arm around her protectively. Then she shrieked to the retreating form, "*You are no mother of mine*!" in much the same tone as Bea had pronounced those selfsame words.

Julius had little time to puzzle over these declarations, or the appearance of this new woman, before he felt himself caught up by the she-beast. Then they both were hit with a violent pulse that made everything go dark.

Daddy!" Beatrix bawled. "No, no, no, Daddy!"

The new woman tried to soothe her. "He's...he's not dead, sweetheart."

"Then where is he? Where did she take him!"

"I don't know, I don't know... but we'll find him."

Bea now shook herself away from this strange new being, moved to a new position, and scrutinized her warily.

"You want to know who I am," said the woman, discerning the younger woman's thoughts. "My manufacturing number was one-four-one-zero."

"I was one-four-one-zero-B."

"The 'halfbreed,'" said the other, but her voice cracked a bit.

"You are...my *mother,*" Bea declared. She declared it matter-of-factly, but her eyes shone with wonderment.

They embraced awkwardly.

"I have been following you, from a distance. Just keeping an eye on you. I didn't want to intrude...I felt it would be ill-advised."

The two women looked upon one another, each unsure of what to say next.

"How did she…how did Mother... I mean, the one we called Mother. How did she...?"

Flabbergasted as she was, Bea found herself unable to articulate her thoughts. The other managed to mutter, "Bilocation. Shape-shifting. The bitch has some talents, I'll give her that much..."

At that moment, both women quite voluntarily turned their gaze towards the spot where the person who had gone under the guise of Deborah, or "the Mayor," a feisty lady from the heartland with a tragic past," had betrayed her true form mere moments ago, and had somehow absconded into thin air, taking Julius with her.

Suddenly, Bea began to weep uncontrollably.

"Daddy! I want my daddy!" she cried out with the primal grief of a child, as the horrifying realization of Julius's absence made itself known to her full apprehension.

The older woman seized her up and embraced her as her body convulsed with violent, seizure-like sobs.

"My dear child, we will find him," she muttered, with a firm undertone of conviction. And in spite of herself, to feel her own daughter in her own grasp at last brought quite incongruent tears of joy to her own eyes.

We must here address the heretofore unaccounted for tale of the member of the Lilith Line who was assigned the title of "1410," the one who inexplicably gave birth to our girl "Bea," whose name was a self-chosen derivation of the title they gave her, anomalous being that she was, having become the progeny of a member (namely "Lilith Unit 1410") of a species of clone explicitly designed to be infertile.

One might, if one were so inclined, inquire about the esoteric significance of the seemingly random number of this particular clone's designation. The author must admit that he is not one given to considerations of numerology, yet in this case he feels somehow honor bound to address this matter, however briefly.

One might consider that one plus four plus one plus zero equals six, which in many esoteric circles is considered a number which denotes imperfection, or rather that which falls just short of perfection. Seven, by contrast, is the *perfect* number, the one denoting divinity and sublimity. This is why seven is often seen as God's number, while Satan is represented by six. The latter, being a magnificent being in his initial incarnation as God's "light-bearer," became fatally enraptured by his own glory, forgetting that his wondrous beauty was but a pale reflection of the one who had created him; thus, he fell spectacularly due to his overweening pride and lust for power. His singular desire to dethrone his Creator and take His place proved to be his eternal undoing.

Lilith Unit 1410, then, might have won her "name," esoterically speaking, by having been "created" to manifest beauty, femininity, and simultaneous innocence and sensuality, though in truth all of these sublime qualities she seemed to radiate so involuntarily were counterfeit, both in the sense that her being was merely a facsimile of an actual person (i.e., a clone), but also, and perhaps more significantly, in the sense that the acts she was trained to perform (namely, seduction, murder, and the threatened ruination of reputations to create blackmailable assets) savored of nothing blessed or holy whatsoever.

Contrarily, one might take the numerological tack of multiplying, rather than adding, the numbers of her given designation, in which case we have the following configuration: one times four equals four, times one equals four, times zero equals zero, for the overall total of zero.

In this case, the esoteric interpretation may run as follows: while Lilith Unit 1410 seemed by all appearances, to be not merely a human being, but one of the most desirable human beings imaginable, in truth she was nothing human at all, but an utter non-entity, a "zero."

Yet, amazingly, this "zero," who was designed to be used and then thrown onto the scrap heap once her utility had ceased, had, over the course of carrying out the "work" she had been assigned by her masters, somehow managed to conceive a child. Such an event could only be called a miracle, even by those within the inner circle of the Lilith operation.

The decision was made to allow the pregnancy to be carried to term, and for the child to be taken away for special scrutiny. After all, given that Unit 1410 had been the one chosen for her task of the "Beastmaker" project (involving the discovery of the "man of wrath" appropriate for the task of impregnating Mother herself, in order that the prophecy of the "Son of Wrath" could reach fulfillment, bringing about the Great Cleansing and finally the Restoration of the Beast), it only made sense that she would display unique qualities, though none had expected that she would actually manifest them in so radical a manner.

Still, as her very existence might augur something relevant and needful, Mother chose to keep the child around. The story of this "halfbreed's" miserable young life and eventual escape has already been recounted. As for her mother, she was never the same after gaining the knowledge of having a daughter. Though her captors had induced a coma-like state, in order that she might not be conscious at the moment of birth, she nevertheless became aware, an innate level, that *something* had been taken from her while she was out, and that that something wasn't actually a "thing" at all, but a baby...namely, *her* baby.

When Mother, known to the world outside of the Lilith Lab as Eveline

Agatha Crumple, appraised Unit 1410 of the situation, she evidently expected Unit 1410 (henceforward to be known as Fourteen) to put the entire notion of motherhood out of mind, since her child would henceforth be kept out of her sight. In spite of the miraculous conception and birth that had resulted from her assigned tryst with Dr. Jude Omega, Mother seemingly dismissed the very idea that Fourteen even had the capacity to feel maternal urges, such as a wish to be reunited with her daughter and shield her from harm.

Fourteen grasped that Mother had underestimated her, since he dismissed the humanity of all of the Lilith units, seeing them as mere instruments, to be used, then discarded when no longer useful. She assumed that they were simply pre-programmed machines, incapable of experiencing complicated human emotions. Upon recognizing these things about Mother, Fourteen grasped that her best strategy would be to do nothing to dissuade her from such misconceptions. Instead, she would merely go about her business, doing what she was told, continuing to be a worthwhile "instrument," while all the while biding her time, attempting to find a means of escape for both herself and for Bea.

"It was so difficult," Fourteen recalled. "But then again, they had trained us to be deceptive, hadn't they? So I just used my training against them."

As the years went by, Fourteen continued to be one of the most effective assets of all of the Liliths. Even as she aged past the point when most units were believed to have lost their effectiveness, she continued to shine. She carried out many a seduction/blackmail mission with many a prominent man and woman, providing Mother and her superiors with needful intelligence time and again.

During all of that time, she carefully tuned her psychic antenna, in an effort to locate the presence of her daughter. One evening, she felt she had struck paydirt, but her elation was immediately tempered by sorrow and anger; her awareness of Bea's consciousness made her fully aware of the misery of her life. She became aware that her daughter was, in fact, lost in a wilderness of pain, and crying out-- as one often cries out in the wilderness-- for a supportive voice.

Immediately, Fourteen began whispering gentle messages of encouragement. Having been gifted with certain dreams of the future, she let her daughter know that she would have to suffer trials, but that eventually a man would appear to save her, one that she would afterwards know as "father." She also let her know that her true mother lived, and that she loved her very much.

"That... was you?" Beatrix's eyes were widened with wonder. "I had cried out for someone to help me.."

"I know," the other woman said, in a rueful tone, her eyes moistening with tears. "I heard you, my daughter. I heard."

The two women embraced again, this time with great familiarity, as if they had known one another for years, each of them sobbing with a shared joy so intense it bordered on grief.

Over the course of the next few days, Fourteen told Bea the rest of her story. After the fateful evening in which the newly elected Senator had been killed and his "son" had been conceived by a drugged, dazed Julius, the same evening in which Julius had recovered his wits, beat Crumple to death, rescued Bea, and absconded into the woods with her, Mother had given the order that the Lilith Lab be shut down. "It has achieved its purpose, and it is time to move on to the next phase of the plan," she had told the Lilith staff. She assured them all that they would be reassigned to other projects, and not face unemployment.

"What about the girls?" asked one man.

"It was the same man," Fourteen said, "whom I had heard, when everyone thought I was asleep, declaring my birth 'a miracle of sorts,' before adding, quite meekly, to Mother, 'I'm sorry, ma'am, I was raised Catholic.'"

"We all have hurdles to overcome," Mother had answered him, quite sententiously, on that occasion. Yet his words had clearly affected her concerning the likely significance of Unit 1410's inexplicable pregnancy. It was the moment when Eveline Crumple had concluded that this as yet unborn child could in fact be an asset to her cause.

But now, several years later, in answer to his question, "What about the girls?" Mother's response had been far more blunt. "The Lilith line will be discontinued. All remaining units are to be put out of operation."

"But ma'am," that man had objected. "Will that not represent a huge loss of investment for us? After all of the gains we have won with the Lilith units?"

"They have performed their assigned tasks well for the past few years, but alas, all good things must come to an end," was Mother's curt retort. Though she used the word "alas," nothing in her tone indicated actual regret.

The man obviously felt crestfallen, though of course he carefully concealed this reaction. He had tried to appeal to Mother via appeals to fiscal responsibility, but the truth was that he had grown fond of "the girls," not just in feeling smitten by their beauty and entranced by their charm, but also because he had grown to view them as patently human, or at least as "human-adjacent" beings.

The man, whose name was Christoph, was clearly struggling with both his libido and his conscience. "I sensed my opportunity," Fourteen said, "but I had to move fast."

Though she wished she could prevail upon his conscience, she was pressed for time. "I had to use the pheromonal enhancements that I had to my own advantage, for once."

So she approached Christoph, took him aside, and forged a bond with him. She prevailed upon him to save her from the planned mass decommissioning of all Lilith units, so that she could be with her daughter again.

"By that time I knew you had escaped, and you were with the man I had seen in my dreams, the one who I knew would save you…"

"Daddy," whispered Bea, starting to get choked up again over the recent loss of the man who had served a paternal role in her life.

"Christoph, bless him, helped me to free me from that infernal institution. I am told that he also rescued other Liliths, though I cannot be sure if that truly happened. But I do know that I owe him my life. His motives weren't totally pure, of course. I think he'd hoped that I would become his lover..."

"Once I got out," she went on, "I found myself overwhelmed by shock. It was so disconcerting to be utterly on my own. Whenever I had departed before to take part in a mission, I was always accompanied by an agent, who kept an eye on me at all times, both to make sure that I accomplished the goal, and—I suspect—to make sure that I didn't try to flee...now, however, I was fleeing. I knew that most of the girls I was leaving behind were being 'decommissioned,' and I felt guilty about leaving them behind;

nevertheless, I didn't dwell on such matters because my main task was finding my daughter...

"I found that you were, for me, a psychic beacon. Wherever you were, I could sense you, like a bloodhound gains a scent. But, my daughter, when I finally found you, and observed you living in such perfect bliss with your father... I somehow couldn't bring myself to intrude. I felt unworthy... Instead, I determined to keep an eye on you, much as my handlers always kept an eye on me... I effectually became your "handler," but with the motive to help, something like a guardian angel... I followed you and your father on your trek, always remaining at a distance.

"Then you arrived here, at Lakeside. I sensed something off about 'Deborah' from the very start, but couldn't be sure what it was. She managed to jam my psychic signals to the point where I couldn't determine her true identity, but all along, I *should* have known...

"I should have known, my daughter," she repeated. "I am sorry."

Once again, she squeezed Bea's hand.

"Take comfort, dear," she whispered. "That beast we called 'Mother' clearly wants your father alive. We will see him again..."

When Julius awoke, he found himself in the room of which he had dreamt when he had glimpsed those images that had provoked such terror and dread in him. Yet the terror and dread were now gone, replaced by a sense of delirious, almost ethereal calm.

Had he been drugged? If so, Julius found that he wanted to become addicted immediately. He had never felt so relaxed, and so relieved, in his life. Vaguely, of course, his mind processed that he had been abducted, that his daughter had been left behind, yet something whispered to him that all was well with Beatrix. Her mother had found her, and would look after her. Julius "knew" this as a deeply held conviction, though of course he had never seen it happen. Was this the effect of the drug (if he was indeed under the influence of something), or did his knowledge spring from some other source?

In any case, Julius was unable to focus on such questions for long, because he found that all remaining sensations of consternation over his situation had dissipated, and sheer, pure bliss now poured into every pore of his being. Joy resounded with each beat of his heart! Why, oh why, had he previously been denied such elation, tempered by such wonderfully mellow undertones?

What was more, the bed in which he now lay, with its soft, cushioned mattress and silky sheets, was far more comfortable than any his body had ever before experienced. Its very contours seemed to caress his frame lovingly, radiating an irresistible impression of supreme luxuriance. After years of sleeping in the wild, there was a voracious thrill to being pampered so expertly.

Julius had never known anything close to happiness in his life.

Eventually, in fact, he had grown reflexively to scoff at the very notion. Though never a religious man, he had long figured, in a vague sort of way, that happiness was reserved for those who had passed on into the next life: Heaven, or Nirvana, or whatever.

But now! In this current mode of being, having been transported to this bed of wondrous comfort, with cascading waves of pleasure flooding his brain, Julius found that he couldn't possibly fathom how Heaven could possibly be any more wonderful than what he was currently experiencing. "Could things ever get better?" he asked himself, unsure if he were actually speaking these words out loud.

As if in answer to his query, a woman of unfathomable beauty suddenly appeared before him, standing at the foot of the bed. Her long hair was raven dark, and she wore a thick fur robe. He hadn't noticed her having entered the room. He knew her from somewhere, yet at the same time felt as though he were beholding her for the very first time. She smiled, pulled off her robe, then tossed aside the covers that had shrouded his body, causing Julius to realize that he too was naked. As she straddled him, his body involuntarily responded to the contact and in no time he was inside her, after which the raven-haired beauty began to undulate, with nimble precision, upon his now thoroughly awakened hardware.

They locked eyes, and he saw her smile transform into an intense open-mouthed pant; she licked her lips and her eyeballs rolled back, like a woman immersed in a trance; he felt her nether region grow sticky and dewy, and suddenly, obeying an unspoken demand, he flipped her over, bestrode her loins, reversing their prior position; in response, the raven-haired woman howled with feral delight as he gripped her back and drove himself into her a with fierce abandon... Something inside of him suddenly wanted to wreck her utterly, to give her immense pain, to break her from within; he trust harder and harder and as she flung her head back and her continuous climax cascaded over his crotch, he fantasized that he was plunging his fleshly rapier ever deeper into her frame; he saw, as if it were truly happening (was it?), the blood spurt in torrents from the ever-growing gash he was ripping into her middle; then he was seizing her legs, pulling them further and further apart until the tendons tore and she screamed and lurched about as one in her death throes and he continued to drill into her midsection, finally reaching her intestines, and then her heart, which his ruthless thrusts now pierced and shattered; finally, knowing that he had finished her off, he released his own load directly into that now thoroughly desiccated organ of hers, desecrating her insides with his climax, which he made sure to spray everywhere, so that her wretched corpse would bear his mark from proverbial stem to stern...

Then he collapsed next to her spent and defiled body. He closed his eyes, and wondered for a moment just what had been real and what had been illusory. He hated her, for reasons that he vaguely recalled, yet he also desired her with what seemed like an eternal fire burning within him.

Finally, she groaned with the same feral intonation as before, and he knew that somehow, though it had all assuredly been (in some sense) real, even still she had survived his relentless assault, and, what is more, had thoroughly enjoyed it.

"Oh, *fuckboy,*" she muttered, in a tone of reverent regard. "Yes, I felt that. Every bit of it. Oh my dear, dear man of wrath, it has been so long. It has been worth the wait..." She rolled over, pulled his face close to hers, kissed him gently. "Do you not remember our last time together?"

He flashed back to that occasion, in the back of her limousine, where they had entangled with primal abandon, though not entirely with his consent; still, once she started in on him, he found himself unable to fight her off. She had taken him as surely as any rapist, but he had nevertheless reached his orgasm at the same time as he had hers, and at that moment of mutual release she had for just a split second revealed her true, frightening form.

Faintly, Julius felt a tingle of apprehension at the memory, along with other events of that evening filled with appalling depravity. He recalled how Evan Crumple had assaulted Beatrice, had leapt atop her with his disgusting naked body, before Julius, infused with fury, had grabbed him and smashed him to a pulp with little more than his bare hands. Additionally, he had crushed the face of a Lilith unit who had attempted to aid and abet Crumple's effort to "crucify" the girl—as he considered her a useless manifestation of the "flesh" and himself a stalwart defender of a higher and more exalted "spirit."

He had taken both of them out with brute force, charged from within by that infernal rage that had possessed him from an early age, gripped and seized him and had barely allowed him relief, had eventually impelled him towards a determination of self-extinguishment: a task which he had almost succeeded at accomplishing before they pulled him away, drugged him up, and institutionalized him.

"They couldn't keep it under wraps, though, could they, fuckboy?" the woman asked. "It was your superpower!"

In a flash, yet still not fully comprehending, Julius remembered that he had been on the brink of killing this appalling woman, in that wretched basement which smelt of death in that awful mansion of demonic depravity. Yet just as he started in on her, she warned him that she was now carrying his child, which had been conceived in the limo a few hours earlier

"You *remember,*" she whispered, stroking his back gently. "Oh man of wrath, you privileged me with your seed."

"So long ago," he muttered. A new sensation was building up inside of him, equally as pleasurable, but more energetic. He had so enjoyed tearing this woman literally in half; now, seeing her somehow intact, he wanted to do it again.

"Go ahead," she goaded. "You were made for wrath. Why should you restrain yourself from that which comes to you naturally?"

But just then a thought seized him. She spoke of his "seed," and he flashed back to his anxiety-soaked nightmares.

"Where is my son?" he asked her.

She smiled enigmatically at him, which he found infuriating. He knew she was baiting him, and that he ought to resist, but right now, he just didn't care. Instead, he yielded to the bloodlust which had flared up again, and drove his fist into her face several times, in quick succession. Her nose busted with what was for him a highly satisfying snap, and blood flooded from her nostrils to the pillow case, staining the immaculate bedspread.

She looked up at him, spat out a tooth, and spoke: "You can do this all you want, fuckboy. Kill me over and over and over again. And I will keep returning for you to murder me anew..."

Tempted as he felt to ravage her again, in a manner still more grotesquely thoroughgoing than before, he held back, and asked again, with greater emphasis, *"Where is my son?"*

She looked up at him, grinning insolently as blood continued to leak from her nose and mouth.

"Our son, darling fuckboy. He is advancing to his rightful ascendant position, thanks be to you and your needful seed."

Then she abruptly got up, and still bloody and naked, took his hand and steered him into an adjoining room. There an enormous telescreen, with the volume turned down, bore the following headline: "EVAN CRUMPLE JR. LEADING BY DOUBLE DIGITS IN ALL PRESIDENTIAL POLLS." At the top Julius beheld a strapping, youthful lad clad in an impeccably-tailored suit standing behind a podium, addressing a crowd.

Eveline pressed a button on the wall, and the volume was activated. Now, Julius heard the lad speak, in a mellifluous voice, one which expressed itself authoritatively yet at the same time betrayed a hint of disarming guilelessness. The voice sounded hauntingly familiar.

"We will restore our country to peace and prosperity!" he was declaring. "We will cast out those oligarchs and warmongers and liars and thieves and rapists who have plagued our ruling so-called elite! We will send them all to Hell, where they belong!" A roaring tide of enthusiastic assent went up

"He sounds like *you,*" Eveline whispered in his ear, but she needn't have: Julius was already thinking that exact thing.

"He is our rightful conqueror. 'He will rule them with an iron scepter, and dash them all to pieces like pottery.'" She gazed upon her son with intense reverence. "Behold, I am the new Eve, and you, dear fuckboy, are my Adam. Together we have conceived another Cain, yet unlike the Cain of ancient days, he will not merely slay his brother, but will burn down the world, cleanse the filth, after which there shall come forth a new Eden..."

Julius, however, barely heard her, so entranced was he by the sight of the young man who stood before the adoring throng on the telescreen. Was this truly his own son? There were certain features that unmistakably favored his mother. All genes relevant to beauty had clearly been passed to him from his mother, yet the way he stood, the way he talked, the expressions he conveyed uncannily recalled Julius himself, albeit a version of Julius possessed of greater charisma and confidence.

"He is the best of both of us," Eveline muttered softly, as if tuned into his thoughts. "But the wrath that animates him, that is entirely his father's."

His firebrand peroration completed, the lad now made his way down through the crowd, slapping high fives and giving fist bumps to a sea of outstretched hands as they reached out to him like imperiled passengers desperately seeking survival from a tempestuous sea raging all around them. He met their flailing limbs with the surehandedness of one who not only held to the confidence of his abilities, but who also knows in his soul that the efforts he intends upon undertaking are preordained, even written in the stars.

Witnessing him for the very first time, Julius felt an odd combination of pride and fear.

"He's *more* than either one of us," he whispered. "He's something totally his own."

"Yes. He's more than *all* of us," she whispered back. She took his hand, and momentarily looking over, he absently registered that, once again, in spite of his most recent assault, her face was no longer bloody. Once more, she had initiated her newly-acquired abilities. He did not resist her touch, much as he loathed and despised her, due to the wondrous vision his eyes and ears were taking in. He knew that he and Eveline Agatha Crumple had each contributed to bringing this wonderful being, this exalted entity, into existence. He thus sense himself bonded with this dreadful woman, little as he wished to be. But under the circumstances, how could things be otherwise?

The presidential election that year followed a significantly different trajectory than ever before.

The last several iterations of this dismal American leap year ritual had each become more drearily predictable than the last.

Always, there was a ratcheting up of hot-button "culture war" issues. Outrage abounded. People were at one another's throats in no time. It became supremely wearying almost instantly. Apocalyptic scenarios were feverishly pitched by partisans of each candidate if the "other side" were allowed to win. The phrase *"most important election ever"* was repeatedly invoked by pundits, podcasters, and talking heads. People who already dealt with a great deal of stress in their day-to-day lives were wound up to the point of snapping. Everyone in their hearts just wanted it to be over, already, so that some semblance of normalcy could return, but they nevertheless continued to play-act their roles as supporters of Candidate A or Candidate B, allowing the overall grotesque spectacle to metastasize further.

Election hubbub became like a negative addiction for many. Negative in the sense that, unlike even deeply unhealthy drug addictions, it brought absolutely no pleasure, only strife of spirit. Even if the candidate you favored wound up "winning," once the votes were all ostensibly "counted," you had the possibility of post-election chicanery to vex your thoughts. The seemingly losing candidate might succeed at bringing suit charging fraud, or electoral voters could be dissuaded or blackmailed to turn against their own candidate.

Even after one candidate or the other was actually finally sworn in on Inauguration Day (which seemed to roll around only after an eternity had elapsed), things never truly felt "over." Little effort was ever made to make the half of the nation who had voted against the winning candidate feel like they belonged within the new paradigm of power; thus, alienation festered, ramified, multiplied, amongst the "loser" half of the voting public.

Though few would admit it, the widespread sentiment was that presidential elections were a bother, a source of needless consternation, strain, and heartache. Whoever "won," it seemed that things changed little, if at all. In spite of the dire prognostications of doomsday scenarios should the "bad" candidate prevail rather than the "good" one, doomsday failed to materialize. Instead, excepting a few generally cosmetic changes, the status quo was always maintained, as if by the steadfast intervention of some invisible hand.

Indeed, the status quo managed to prevail, even as great and terrible events seized the headlines and shook an already fragile "union" into further upheaval. In fact, the status quo only continued down its dismal trajectory, regardless of who happened to "win" the last election. Wars for supposed "freedom" were declared and waged in Eastern Europe and the Far East, against nations that did not in fact pose any sort of danger to the United States. There were constant threats to reinstate the draft, keeping everyone on edge. Still worse was the enforced resettlement of much of the rural population to the cities, in the name of the federal government's UN-mandated "green initiative."

The latter campaign, even more than the seemingly never-ending interventionist wars in foreign lands, created the most upheaval. Those who denounced what came to be called "Trail of Tears 2.0" attempted to bring suit, but this effort ultimately failed when the Supreme Court voted 6-3 that the notion of removing people from their native homes and resettling them in massive squalorous campsites near major cities was in fact NOT unconstitutional, since the ongoing crisis of "climate change" unfortunately necessitated the taking of such drastic measures.

"While the Constitution may not explicitly mention environmental emergencies as a cause for the suspension of certain 'rights' for a temporary interval," the majority opinion declared, *"it is also true that the Founding Fathers had no conception of an situation like the one faced by humanity today, where an existential matter like climate change threatens the very future of the planet..."* Later, it was pointed out by some brave independent

journalists that each and every one of the majority of Justices had, to a man or woman, been bought out by powerful corporate-created entities, which favored the instituting of the resettlement initiative. Of course, these reports were immediately suppressed under the "Misinformation Prevention Act," which had been narrowly passed by Congress and signed into law by the president whose Cabinet occupied the White House prior to the current one (a president who, interestingly, had been the supposedly "conservative" choice).

The minority opinion representing opposition to the resettlement initiative expressed *"deep concern"* about the fact that people *"would be forcibly uprooted from their rightful homes"* by the initiative, and averred that *"great mischief will likely result from this egregious action, unprecedented since the removal of the Cherokees from the southeast in the early 19th Century in the 'Trail of Tears,' a campaign that has since been universally condemned for its cruelty and utter inhumanity."* Yet, at the same time, they sternly admonished citizens who opposed the measure to *"eschew violence"* and *"obey the injunction, because citizens of a law-abiding nation must act lawfully in any and all circumstances."*

The minority opinion struck many as unforgivably tepid, causing some to wonder if the three dissenting justices were only playing the part of "symbolic" or "controlled" opposition. In any case, it was, to use that ever-ubiquitous golfing metaphor, par for the course. A demoralized population prepared for even greater indignities to be visited upon them. Heartland dwellers cast about for leaders to speak up on their behalf, but found to their dismay that the majority of conservative-leaning authority figures whom they tended to respect, seemed loathe to do anything but advise compliance and discourage active resistance. "Violence only begets violence," one famous ex-professor counseled, somewhat sententiously, his distinctive high-pitched voice rising with emotional conviction. "The policy is, to be sure, heinous," declared a much-loved podcaster, "but to instigate force against our own National Guard personnel who are carrying out the resettlement order would be treasonous."

"Brothers and sisters in the affected regions of our nation," spoke one world-famous preacher, "who now find themselves being targeted for this deeply misguided so-called 'resettlement' plan, we pray earnestly on your behalf. What you are being subjected to is an obscenity. But let us not compound the wickedness already being done by plotting any death or destruction towards the noble men and women of the National Guard, who are, after all, only carrying out their orders...let us show our fundamental decency as law-abiding Christians by adhering to the letter of the law, even when the law is totally unjust."

Indeed, no high-profile self-described "conservative" was eager to oppose the resettlement campaign, which went under the official title of the "Save the Planet" Initiative, or SPI. Instead, as if with one voice, they all sternly counseled obedience, and forbade what they labeled "insurrection."

When violence did break out, as would only be expected, given the circumstances, and people quite understandably attempted to defend themselves against forced resettlement, resulting in injury and death to some of the armed forces who had been sent to compel their expulsion from their homes, the high-profile "conservatives" were the first to condemn these "maimings and murders" and to demand that those responsible for such "capital crimes" be harshly punished "to the full letter of the law, and beyond."

When some in the "resettlement zone" refused to leave their homes, and used arms to attempt to repel their "resettlers," these incidents were indeed used as fodder for anti-rural propaganda. How dare these backwoods rednecks commit such outrages against what was a good, just, and proper campaign to save the planet? Liberal-leaning urban dwellers, who had been persuaded by years of propaganda to think of themselves as morally superior to their fellow citizens who dwelt in smaller towns, i.e., to view them as stupid hicks who talked like uneducated rubes and clung to prejudices and their guns and attended their abominable houses of worship which promoted dangerous superstitions, etc., soon became avid promoters of resettlement. Many posted on social media to the effect that the National Guardsmen were being entirely too lenient, that resettlement ought to give way to arbitrary firing squads and the digging of mass graves. "These backwards sub-humans hickazoids have shown themselves to be lives unworthy of life. Kill them all! Let them feed the trees and the plants..." asserted one poster. He received numerous upvotes (downvotes had long ago been removed, to prevent bullying or "organized gangstalking" by "Russian bots"). Other similar posts were likewise well-received by a broad swath of likeminded social media denizens, whose murderous rage against the so-called "hickazoids" had reached a feverish intensity.

Occasional rumors (floated mostly by "non-approved" sources, deemed automatically to be "misinformation" by ever-zealous "fact-checkers") made reference to occasions in which certain atrocities were in fact committed by National Guardsmen against citizens, including the reported mass execution of 24 men, women, and children in a tiny homesteading community called Sanctuary, located in western Ohio. Apparently, at least according to these "unapproved" sources, the "Sanctuary martyrs," as they came to be known in some circles, were put to death in an especially heinous manner, which included the alleged rape of the women and girls while the men and boys (their husbands, sons, and brothers, and fathers) were forced to watch, after which the entire group was remorselessly gunned down and their bodies set aflame, along with the entirety of their homesteading establishment. Their livestock—mostly pigs and chickens—were thereafter burned alive in the conflagration and perished with awful squawks and screams of torment.

The Sanctuary slaughter ostensibly took place because beleaguered Guardsmen were frustrated and ground down by months mired in combat with recalcitrant citizens, the so-called "bitter enders," who put up fierce armed resistance, resulting in the deaths and injuries of scores of soldiers. Many Guardsmen, their hearts made bitter by the relentless slog of their thankless mission, then ostensibly felt the urge, in the words of a whistleblower, "to send a message to these redneck pukes that we mean business."

The story, and the quote, was allegedly leaked by one of the Guardsmen involved in the atrocity, who could not shake the sounds of the tormented beasts and birds as they were scorched alive, nor could he forget the screams of the girl he had raped, while her mother wept and pleaded for mercy, none of which had prevented him from climaxing inside the girl and beating her head in with a rock immediately afterwards. ("That girl couldn't have been older than 13," he muttered, as if awed and frightened by his own brutality, a stranger which had malignantly manifested within his own skin to commit such savage deeds.)

The "Sanctuary" story was, of course, immediately dismissed as "misinformation." Those ubiquitous "fact-checkers" declared it to be baseless, a mere rumor, spread by deeply untrustworthy people. Major newspapers and magazines, both of the print and online variety, ran articles sternly condemning "the Sanctuary slander" as "a lurid, far-right fever dream." Yet in spite of the best efforts of the "respectable" media to suppress the story or to associate those who believed it with racism, sexism, homophobia, fascism, and other undesirable mindsets and ideologies, it nevertheless continued to spread. The newly-passed misinformation law (discussed above), which put those who knowingly spread accounts deemed to be false by the authorities in danger of severe fines or even imprisonment, meant that news of the "Sanctuary massacre" had to be "whispered" surreptitiously, or voiced on unofficial and unlicensed channels, which managed to operate outside of the orbit of the approved media control grid.

The Sanctuary story proved to be the spark that ignited a long-simmering fuse amongst a large subsection of the populace who were deeply unhappy with the overall direction things had taken. Street protests, many of which accumulated thousands of people, were organized in numerous cities. These demonstrations were almost completely ignored by the major media, and the brutal manner with which riot police put down these unarmed protesters, often with live bullets, resulting in an unknown number of casualties, likewise went unremarked upon and unreported, at least from "official" news outlets. Still, word got around by other means, and discontent and dissension continued to roil the populace.

"Avenge Sanctuary!" became a catchphrase amongst those outraged by the resettlement campaign, and the atrocities increasingly being reported, in defiance of the consortium of "fact checkers" being relentlessly dispatched by state- and corporate-affiliated venues. With Sanctuary, the power-brokers and cultural opinion-shapers eventually came to see that they had foundered upon a stumbling block, one which threatened to sink them. How to proceed? Some insiders advised that official sources own up to the horrific events of Sanctuary, but make clear that this was the behavior of wayward soldiers who would be brought before a tribunal and punished harshly for their crimes. That way, the power-brokers and opinion-shapers could claim that the resettlement program in itself was a worthy enterprise, but that "a few bad apples" had unfairly tainted the effort. But others strongly urged against such a course of action, claiming that it would have the effect of making the current administration appear "defensive" and would put them "back on their heels," giving dissidents the upper hand, a circumstance which must be avoided at all costs.

So the Sanctuary story continued to spread, and outrage festered, both in the hinterlands and in the metropolises. City life, after all, had grown ever more intolerable. Cameras were everywhere, and utterances against the behavior of the increasingly encroaching surveillance state were often caught on strategically planted detection devices, resulting in numerous citizens finding themselves hit with fines for "publicly spreading misinformation" when their faces were recognized in the population database; such fines would be sent via text or email at first, and if ignored, an ominous looking letter with red coloring (referred to sardonically by many as "a Valentine from the government") would arrive in their mailbox, warning that if the payment weren't made promptly, "further action would be taken."

Then, one evening, an event transpired which sent shock waves through a largely jaded populace, and provoking panic amongst many who dwelt in those proverbial "high places" in the nation's capital and elsewhere.

A then little-known individual, a young man born under tragic circumstances nearly two decades ago, made his first appearance in an interview with on a certain well-known "semi-dissident" vlogcast. The labels "semi-dissident," or, still more scathingly, "pseudo-dissident" had been coined by many to describe the sort of "conservative" commentator who claimed to oppose the SPI resettlement program, but habitually scolded those who proposed those being forcibly resettled doing anything whatsoever to defend themselves or prevent themselves from being forcibly uprooted.

On this particular date, this vlogcast host, with seemingly little if any foreknowledge concerning the momentousness of the occasion, booked Evan Crumple Jr. The world had seen little of him prior to this point; none could have guessed that he was a weapon kept carefully concealed, and that, after years of waiting patiently, the deployers of this weapon had finally opted to pull the trigger.

The interview began innocuously enough. Viewers were treated to the sight of this youngster, who gazed at the host with a countenance so placid that it seemed plain uncanny. When the host inquired about what it was like to grow up under the shadow of his father, a man regarded as a "genuine reformer" before he was tragically murdered by an unstable staffer before Evan Jr. was even born, the lad's gaze shifted abruptly; his eyes turned steely, and his voice was heard for the first time.

"My father died for the sake of truth. I am here to pick up the mantle and bring it to its proper conclusion."

The phrase "proper conclusion" gave the host significant pause. To him, it sounded "somewhat ominous," he chuckled. In response, Evan Jr. didn't miss a beat. "It should sound ominous to those responsible for our current situation. Their days are numbered."

Evan pronounced these words so calmly that the host was doubly taken aback. In fact, he stammered for a moment, and made an effort to collect himself, before asking just who Evan had in mind when he assailed "those responsible for our current situation." Evan then spoke the words that would later immortalize him among his followers.

"For one thing, anyone pushing the utter abomination that is the so-called "resettlement" currently taking place. Believe me, Sanctuary will be avenged. That's not a threat. It's a promise."

At this point, the host grew alarmed, and attempted to end the interview. However, for some reason the engineer in charge of the feed ignored his boss's frantic gesticulations. The camera remained on Evan, who began to laugh, in a manner that proved to be spectacularly endearing.

"Why ______," he jovially joshed the host, calling him by his first name. "What are you so nervous about?" The camera then inexplicably switched to the host, who was still making throat-cutting motions, a frantic expression on his face.

"You want them to cut the feed, but they won't do it...your engineers now work for me. Yes that's right, I hired them yesterday. We knew this would happen. We knew you wouldn't be able to handle too much truthful talk...why not just have a seat, my friend? We can continue our interview..."

The host, however, got up, flung his headset away, and beat a hasty retreat, looking both furious and comically impotent in the process.

"Now, then, let us continue," Evan said, without missing a beat. "As our host has absconded, I'm afraid that I'll have to do the talking for both of us. But I think I can handle that. Now, then..."

Evan then launched into an impromptu speech, of breathtaking width and scope. He blasted the "purveyors of interventionist foreign wars in the political and corporate elite," declaring that such people "had blood on their hands, both American and foreign." He upbraided the "pushers of economy-destroying lockdowns and worthless, or worth than worthless, vaccines, which far from being 'safe and effective,' are quite manifestly neither safe, nor effective." He raged against the "atrocity of the resettlement effort, and the numerous lives it has disrupted, uprooted, debilitated, ruined, and in many cases, ended."

"There will be a *reckoning* for all of these crimes," he announced. "Those in high places have, for far too long, believed themselves to be untouchable. Let it be known right now: there is *no one,* regardless of the power he may think he enjoys, who is immune from being *touched....*"

The response to the vlogcast was immediate and electrifying.

Who was this young man, barely even an adult, yet possessed of such seeming authority and command? Why had he been "allowed" to speak so boldly what so many were feeling in their hearts, but dared not say aloud, for fear of career ruination, loss of social credit, and even possible fines or jail time?

There was an immediate attempt to retaliate from numerous bastions of the establishment, who editorialized furiously against this mysterious new upstart. Campaigns to bring young Crumple to heel were immediately begun...yet, inexplicably, these efforts never managed to gain traction. Instead, young Crumple's star only continued to rise. Every attempt to counter him foundered. Those who drew attention to his callow youthfulness and absence of experience found themselves rebuked as "toadies" and "enablers of tyranny." Whispering campaigns, alleging various scandalous scenarios concerning young Crumple ("he is a fascist white supremacist who admires Hitler," "he is a bastard child, born of unsavory circumstances," "he engages in unsavory sexual practices, and in fact has often had intercourse with his own mother, who herself is a deviant and cruel woman," among others) were dismissed as scurrilous hearsay. The irony that some of these rumors actually were true made no difference, as truth is rarely a commodity of value in politics.

It wasn't terribly surprising, to those "in the know," that truths were dismissed and that lies prevailed. The sort of people "in the know" in this context, after all, are the very ones spoken of, those who routinely told lies and broadcast them as truth, with great success rates. What was more of a surprise, perhaps even a shock, and highly worrying, if not dismaying, was the suddenly effectual *neutering* of various institutions which had, until now, carried an enormous amount of cultural clout.

That is, it seemed that the political and media machine, which had long played a major role in ferreting out who was worthy of being awarded a seat of power, as opposed to who needed to be immediately drummed out of consideration, was suddenly, staggeringly *impotent.* To be sure, they still published passionately-worded editorials, they still ran acerbic hit pieces, their influencers spared no expense in going on the attack, yet all of the slings and arrows they slung and fired now proved to be duds. None achieved the desired results of making the population question the integrity or credibility of this strange new figure on the cultural scene.

It was the oddest, most disconcerting, most frustrating feeling, to find oneself abruptly deprived of that which one was accustomed to having readily at one's disposal, just as one of a humbler station might count on getting his coffee every morning before work. But now there was no more coffee; the machine had broken and couldn't be repaired. The spigot to the pipeline which supplied the needful juice to these influential institutions and venues had suddenly been shut off. Who had managed to do that?

Again, it wasn't a question of these players, pundits, lobby groups, and influencer organizations ceasing to exist; they simply didn't seem to hold any detectable sway anymore. Had a spell been cast? Or perhaps, just as likely, had an already present spell, long in effect, somehow been broken?

Either way, the effect was the same. The venom and bile of the press towards young Mr. Crumple only resulted in the exponential growth of his popularity. Nobody seemed to care that he was young enough to be a freshman in college. His brazen youth, in fact, only worked in his favor. People grew protective of him, seeing in him a son, or a brother, a best mate, or a potential lover; however they related to him, the attachment rarely manifested as a mere mild or casual acquaintance. Instead, people were moved to tears by his visage. If ever he appeared on a talk show and the host challenged him a bit too stridently, that host would find himself or herself on the receiving end of a barrage of abuse from thousands of outraged viewers. On several occasions, television or Internet personalities felt themselves under intense pressure to apologize for allegedly addressing Evan disrespectfully. Several did, so great was the fear they felt for their safety.

One smirking cable show host who flatly asked Evan, "Why should people vote for you when you're just a little boy?" was immediately greeted with a barrage of loud and lusty boos from his studio audience. For his part, Evan raised a hand to silence his angry supporters, and, with unflappable poise, put forth his answer: "Unless a man become as a little child, he shall not enter the kingdom of Heaven." Then, after a pause, in which his questioner attempted to overcome his bafflement he added, in a slightly more ominous tone, "Do not mistake my youth for cowardice or lack of will. I will ensure that under my watch, things will get done. This is the end of the age of corruption and the dawn of a new eon."

He spoke in a manner that, had one not been watching the screen, would have seemed to issue forth from a much older man, one with sure knowledge of his own authority. It struck the viewer as curiously incongruous to hear one so young pronounce such steely declarations without a trace of artifice. If any other man just barely out of boyhood had spoken these same lines in so solemn a tone, he would have come across as comically out of touch, perhaps even "touched" in the head. At best, he would have brought to mind an actor in a college production, playing the role of a middle-aged father, affecting an unconvincing pompous tone with unconvincing makeup coating his face, aware, perhaps, of the joke all the while.

Yet when young Evan spoke thusly, people marveled at him all the more. Did he have the entire nation under some sort of trance?

A satirical cartoon from a major publication portrayed him as a master hypnotist with eyes like kaleidoscopes; Americans of a certain demographic, namely those backwards, uncouth, backwoods, anti-resettlement types, who were portrayed in a broad and farcical manner; some of them wore "Avenge Sanctuary" T-shirts and had (outrageously enough) swastikas plastered onto their foreheads...as had happened before, the public responded to these derisive cartoons with open violence. The cartoonist received hate mail; his home address and phone number were leaked, and he was assaulted several times in the streets. Eventually, the offending cartoon was pulled. The newspaper was mocked in some quarters for its cowardice, but nationwide polls showed that the overwhelming majority thought the cartoon was grossly unfair and needed to be removed from circulation.

As Election Day grew closer, both of the major parties nominated a candidate. The two candidates, usually bitterly opposed to one another, were in this instance almost in cahoots, desperately trying to find some opportunity to chip away at the massive lead that Evan held in all of the polls. Their highly-paid consultants were, however, at an utter loss. It seemed that none could prevent what was increasingly being viewed as the sheer inevitability of a Crumple victory.

When a debate was staged, both the Democrat and the Republican took turns assailing young Crumple for his ostensibly "atrocious views" (a phrase used by both major party candidates). The Dem took him to task for being a purveyor of "harmful misinformation" and "conspiracy theories," a charge that Evan brushed off with a scoff. "Your boogeyman words have lost all of their power," he replied. "People see right through you, and they don't like what they see so transparently on the inside" (sustained cheers and applause broke out). The Republican then took his turn: "Young man (he began, and was immediately blasted with boos for his cultivated condescension)...you have made some truly abominable statements about the brave and dedicated men and women serving in our armed forces, whether in the capacity of fighting necessary wars against tyranny abroad, or engaging in sadly necessary domestic campaigns in order to preserve the state of our beautiful country from the ravages of climate change..."

"You're talking about the uprooting of citizens from their hometowns, a truly abominable evil, one which I will bring to a swift end once I am leader of this nation," Crumple deftly interrupted. He went on: "I stand by every word I have used to condemn this so-called 'resettlement' atrocity, as well as my insistence upon bringing our troops home from all of the far-flung battlefields around the world, where they are suffering and dying needlessly on a daily basis so that corrupt elites can profit from these needless wars…" (sustained applause and cheers ensued again).

After the debate was over, media outlets did their best to attempt to "spin" the proceedings as an embarrassment for the Crumple campaign. Pundits characterized his responses to the accusations of the other candidates as "snarky and defensive." Some declared that his "immaturity" was on full display, declaring that he came across as "snide and spiteful." But the population seemed to see things otherwise, because after the debate Crumple's favorability quotient only increased, and his poll numbers, already staggeringly high, spiked yet again.

The media pundits then took the tack of attacking the credibility of the polls, insisting that they were inaccurately complied, and hinting that the Crumple campaign was using "dirty tricks" to convince the population that Evan was more popular than he truly was. No actual evidence was marshalled to convincingly demonstrate that such a thing was happening, of course, and the Crumple campaign, for their part, merely shrugged it off. "The media does nothing but lie, why would they stop now?" Crumple asked with the self-assured grin of a man who has just smacked a massive home run and is taking a moment to watch the ball fly into the distant outfield bleachers before trotting a victory lap across the base paths.

Evan Crumple Jr., as it turned out, had every reason to be cocky.

Every allegation flung at him seemed to backfire. When they went after his dear mother, of course, the indignation of Crumple backers was instantaneous and rabid. Just a week before the November election, a scandal piece from a highly-placed tabloid with an alleged "anonymous insider" as its ostensible source claimed that Evan and his mother had in fact been engaged in a scandalous incestuous relationship for years. Such rumors had made the rounds before, but had failed to gather any momentum; now, the reiteration of these lurid and surely spurious charges caused great fury amongst Evan's more fanatical supporters. The author of the piece remained anonymous, as was his or her claimed source, so a mob just attacked the building which housed the offices of the tabloid in question. All employees were luckily able to escape with no more than minor injuries from the agitators, who broke into the building and ran roughshod over everything; before riot cops could arrive on the scene, they had managed to wreck all of the computers and publishing equipment in the offices, as well as smashing all of the windows, then finally setting the structure ablaze.

The campaigns of both major party candidates, as well as the entirety of the monied media, were incensed by this savage instance of lawlessness; as with one strident, tremulous voice, they called upon Evan to condemn what had taken place. Crumple, however to their astonishment and consternation, did no such thing. "Telling a terrible lie can have terrible consequences," he observed evenly, with no hint of anything resembling regret, remorse, or concern. For her part, Evan's mother spoke in a manner most deemed to be more "responsible," saying she condemned all forms of violence (an irony appreciated by few, as her past remained a secret to all but a few, none of whom dared speak out). Eveline also said that her prayers were with the staff members who had suffered minor injuries, and with the families of everyone affected by the ravages of the rioters.

The would-be puppetmasters, now finding their puppetmastering implements had grown totally ineffective at pulling any strings whatsoever, now attempted one last, desperate gambit. Both the Democrat and the Republican campaigns attempted to cancel the election at the last moment, declaring (through their highly-paid lawyers) a "unique emergency situation, one never faced before in the history of our democracy." The brief, filed before all state and federal courts simultaneously, declared that "in order to protect the freedoms we so cherish as Americans, it is imperative that we postpone these proceedings until some sense of societal equilibrium can be re-established...emotions are running very high right now, fanned by the flames of anger and hatred, and if the past teaches us any lessons, it is that holding an election during a time when anger and hatred run rampant leads to horrific results. Let us do what we must to avert disaster before a once great nation is once again overwhelmed by darkness..."

Every major news journal, both online and offline, wrote editorials heartily endorsing the proposed "indefinite postponement" of the election. Leading actors from Hollywood declared that it would be the best thing for everyone, as did various pop stars. Every possible "influencer" was marshalled, it seemed, in a desperate effort to have the maximum effect upon the populace. Prominent politicians from both parties likewise agreed with the notion that the lawsuit being brought by both parties was "sane, reasonable, and very badly needed," in the words of one aging ex-president. "We are on the precipice of a doomsday scenario," a senior senator warned. "We are treading an unprecedented course," declared a retired newscaster, widely revered for his gentle paternal charm and cautious and prudent centrism.

Numerous others chimed in, yet try as they might, this relentless campaign of "postpone the election" advocates, or "postpone-ists," could do nothing to drown out the roar of the general public, who had grown incensed by this late-minute maneuvering against "their guy." Seemingly spontaneous demonstrations broke out in every city. In Washington, D.C., the demonstrators marched right up to the doorstep of the White House, where National Guard soldiers were promptly positioned. It was widely feared that things would turn bloody, before the news emerged that the Supreme Court had unanimously rejected the suit, on the grounds of "unconstitutionality."

The announcement of the decision caused the assembled crowds to go from angry to jubilant. *"It's on! It's on! It's on! It's on!"* they chanted together, as if with one voice. Newscasters, upon receiving this news, openly displayed their crestfallen countenances. One woman, host of a news network nightly show, even broke down in tears. "It seems that the Crumple campaign has either intimidated, blackmailed, or bought off the highest court in our land," she managed to stutter out, between snivels and sobs. "This is a sad, scary time to be alive..."

The election results, once compiled, surprised no one, though it seemed that many within the echelons of power had hoped for some kind of last-minute intervention to steer the ship of state away from the treacherous waters that surely lay ahead. Yet nothing could prevent that which had seemingly been inevitable all along. What was surprisingly, even shocking, however, was the margin of Evan Crumple's victory. Somewhere around 85 percent of the voting public cast their ballots for the 20-year old independent upstart, with the major party candidates left in the dust to forage pathetically for scraps.

In their concession speeches, both the Democrat and the Republican candidate sounded a tone of alarm. "What we have just seen happen defies understanding," said one of them (it scarcely matters which). "This is the result of people getting exposed to misinformation and a truly toxic culture fed by racism, sexism, and a relentless barrage of paranoid conspiracy theories. Now our new president is a boy who is barely old enough to vote and too young to drink alcohol. And he speaks in all of the lingo of this new subculture, which has now, sadly, become mainstream..."

The other defeated major party candidate (again, one needn't really bother about which of the two he represented), for his part, stated, "Tonight we see the consequences of a reckless and unaccountable culture of ignorance and bigotry..." (he went on in that vein, essentially repeating what his counterpart had said previously, just using slightly different terminology).

But in truth no one cared what the two losers of the election were saying. Instead, a nation reeled, in awe of the event which had actually transpired, an event in which they had all in some way participated, yet little understood.

In the week prior to Evan's inauguration, a curious event took place, one which was all the more curious in that no one noted it at the time. Even afterwards, when it became a matter of hot debate, few connected it with the extraordinary events that had befallen the nation.

What happened was one of those phenomena that have come to be known as another instance of the "Mandela effect," when a collective memory from the recent past reveals itself to be apparently false. A children's book that you grew up with, for example, knowing all the while that the title bore a particular name, only to find out as an adult that its name had in fact always been different, in spite of the fact that millions of other people recall the same divergent title as yourself, and those millions can hardly all be dismissed as delusional...

Other memories, usually involving things related to popular culture (famous lines in movies, advertising logos, and the like), i.e., from sources that draw from a collective consciousness, are, in the case of the "Mandela effect," also suddenly and inexplicably different, yet we are told (again) that these differences have always been what they are now, much as our recollections clearly tell us otherwise. Even Bible verses are not immune from this disturbing and uncanny occurrence. (Apparently, for example, there is no Old Testament prophecy of a time when "the lion shall lay down with the lamb," the lion mentioned in the verse in question now having been inexplicably replaced by a wolf...)

Just as with these previous instantiations, where at some point in time much of the population is shocked to discover that something they had always known to be true in fact had seemingly always been otherwise, so the new and startling "Mandela effect" washed over the world's consciousness just as young Evan Crumple was preparing to assume the reins of power in the United States of America. That is, it suddenly became true, and after the pattern of "Mandela effect" events elsewhere, it had apparently *always* been true, that Earth had two moons, not just one.

One of Earth's moons, that is, was the one which is most often thought of as the Moon, was the silvery-gray disk which could be seen by the naked eye on most clear nights, at least during its phases of visibility. But (and this was the bit of information that many people didn't realize that always been true), there was *another* object, roughly one-fourth the size of the "main" Moon, which kept up an orbit around the Earth which was much more rapid than its larger, fellow satellite. Stories emerged (but in fact they had always been told, apparently) about how the astronauts on manned Moon missions had to plot a course that would be sure to "miss" the smaller mass which kept such a relentless pace, completing its circle of the Earth in just slightly longer than once a day.

No plan had ever been made to land on the smaller moon, titled "Hermes" for the speed at which it hurtled around Earth, on account of its composition apparently being something more akin to "slime" than rock. Hermes also assumed a deep green color, quite a vivid contrast with the duller-complexioned "main" Moon, which curiously had no name other than "the Moon," as if there weren't another, as if the streaking emerald flash of slimy consistency weren't truly just as much of a satellite as its more distant and lugubriously-paced counterpart.

Hermes (it was now understood) existed. Hermes had in fact *always* existed. Hermes had long been called "Hermes," while for some reason "the Moon" had never been given any name other than "Moon," which is sort of like a person having a name like "Person." Such was now the acknowledged reality on the day when Evan Crumple was sworn in as "President," a title which in fact he had never once used during his candidacy, and which, once it was bestowed upon him, he promptly and unceremoniously discarded.

"I am not your President," he stated baldly in his inauguration speech. "I am your Leader, and I am here to do the will of the one who sent me...I am not a man, I am dynamite. I am an avenging fire, I am the swift blade of Justice, I am the scourge of the unrighteous. I will visit havoc upon all those in high places who have feasted upon the innocent. They will pay, and pay dearly, for the crimes they have committed!"

A roar went up from the assembled throng, which packed the mall area of Washington, D.C. and surrounding districts in record numbers. Never had anyone heard an Inauguration address like this, one which sounded more like the unrestrained oratory of an Old Testament prophet instead of consisting of the same contrived, carefully rehearsed, test-marketed talking points of a typical politician. A few eyebrows were raised by such a spectacle, but all who found the scene discomfiting—not only President Crumple's words, but the fact that their articulator, Crumple himself, was a college-aged youth, who nevertheless spoke so authoritatively, after the manner of an elder, and that, moreover, he spoke so freely of the notion of visiting *retribution* and *bloodshed* upon the "unrighteous"—were in the minority, and many, in truth, had undeniably self-interested reasons to be discomfited.

The newly sworn-in President, who declaimed the very title of "President," then did something most extraordinary. He looked to the sky for a long moment, and declared, "There, behold Hermes! Our faithful satellite...visible to us now, even by daylight, an emerald orb just above our atmosphere...it streaks across our world, never stopping to pause, never needing to rest! Note Hermes well, friends. I am Hermes in the flesh. But unlike our companion in the sky, I shall crash into this Earth, and topple the mighty from their high places...I will set the Earth ablaze with flames that will burn and burn and burn, and never be consumed. The Great Reckoning is here! The Storm is upon us!"

Full-throated cheers greeted this final declaration, cheers so deafeningly loud they might well have been issuing from the depths of the Earth. Buoyed up by the crowd's unrestrained adulation, Evan raised his arms and balled his fists, an Olympian receiving fire from the heavens.

No human eyes, save those of the two persons involved, saw what happened mere moments later, after Evan stepped off the dais and excused himself momentarily, entering a side room furnished with a couch and a mirror, and closing the door.

The 20-year-old newly-elected commander-in-chief gazed intently into his own eyes, attempting to still, or at least stabilize, the roiling passions now churning within him. Delivering speeches always left him feeling intoxicated, yet also energized, almost to the point of being manic. Though possessed of a sense of mission that only grew stronger and more intense every day, Evan Crumple Jr. also had an ever-evolving understanding of what that mission involved. Things had been coming into ever-greater focus lately. Now was the time; the die was cast; the Rubicon had been crossed. He smiled at himself, nodded, felt utterly at peace with what must be done.

Presently the door behind him opened. Evan had been expecting this, and didn't bother to turn around. There came the sound of a match striking, and a cigarette being lit. Evan closed his eyes.

"Mother," he whispered. It was half a greeting, half a plea.

"Mr. President," she answered, after taking a perfunctory puff.

When he said nothing, she stepped closer. His eyes were still closed, yet he could see her face, animated by extreme ecstasy, which already bordered on orgasmic. He opened his eyes, turned, and beheld her visage. Her smile, it turned out, was even broader than he had imagined it in his mind's eye. She gripped his right shoulder with her left hand, and took another, longer drag from the lit cig in her right. Then she put it into his mouth, and made him take a puff before dropping and crushing it beneath a stiletto heel.

He looked her up and down, frowning slightly. "You didn't have to dress so provocatively, Eveline. It's unseemly. You're a head of state's mother."

"Afraid I would upstage you?" she asked, coyly. Then she kissed him roughly on the mouth, and he, though at first startled, and put off by the smoke which saturated her oral cavity, presently returned her affections with some zeal. He kissed her back forcefully, gripped her tightly, felt his desire mount quickly. How often, during his youthful years, had she suddenly flung herself at him with unabashed lust and demanded satiation? When he had been very young, her advances had frightened him; as he advanced into adolescence, he came to accept the liberties she took with him as a matter of course. This is not to say that he wasn't aware, from the start, that he was being violated in the worst possible way; in fact, he always comprehended this, even if his awareness was merely inchoate at first...

Their trysts had continued, not on a daily basis (which would have rendered them monotonous), but often enough that he grew wary and learned to associate his own arousal with that same sense of wariness. Her abuse had rendered him helplessly habituated; he became his mother's lover, came to love and loathe his victimhood with equal measure. He came to know his mother's body as well as his own, knew what she liked, knew how to do the sort of things to make her go mad with wild, wailing expressions of ecstatic delight.

And all the while, like a host that grows familiar with its parasite, to the point where it sees the very thing sucking the lifeblood out of him as both his nemesis and his treasured soulmate, so his mother's predations worked their insidious charms, causing him to be addicted to her depraved compulsions.

For her part, it seemed, her ardor for him stemmed from some perception of power that she felt he possessed. She had let him know at an early age that the man history taught was his father, the "martyred" senator, was not in fact, the one from whose seed he was conceived. Who was his real father, then? Oh, she said, he was a *man of wrath,* and Evan, his son, would bring what he started to fruition. Unfortunately, the man was dead (so Evan was told), so they would never meet.

Evan had asked her no further questions. He didn't want to seem too eager, didn't want to expose this vulnerability to her. He knew that he must be what she expected him to be. In spite of himself, he wished to please her, pined to live up to the ideal that she had constructed of him.

Now, as he was kissing her in this side room in the Capitol building mere minutes after his inauguration speech, he began to feel in his loins, mingled with the familiar desire, a swiftly unfolding hatred for her.

Her abuse of him had been *wrong*, very *wrong*, and it had twisted him in ways he could barely even understand. But now was the time of Reckoning. He flung his mother to the floor, leapt upon her, tearing her dress off with one mighty yank. He grabbed her breasts, but instead of fondling them, he began to slap them hard; first with a forehand, then with a backhand. He bit her taut right nipple so hard that it bled, then began punching her face. Yet she did not scream; she only sighed and hissed with depraved delight. This enraged him further, and as he rammed into her, his arousal was so pronounced that it immediately tore at her cervix, causing her to gasp with pain. He had never managed to plunge so deeply into her before.

"Do it, do it, *son!* Do it, *Mr. President,*" she implored hoarsely. Enraged, he punched her face again, then thrust again into her, even deeper this time. By now, Eveline was bleeding copiously, both from the nose and between her legs; still, his continued plunges into her continued unabated; it now felt to her as if he were invading *her very being,* the same way that he had at that moment of conception so long ago, when she had first felt him quickening in her womb...

"This...is...your...*reckoning*...Mother!" he gasped out, between murderous thrusts. "You... made. . .me...be...like...*this*. . .now...*die!*"

At her savage pronouncement of that last word, Eveline and her son both climaxed abundantly; he pulled himself out of her just in time to hear her guttural death rattle before her body stiffened and her breathing ceased.

At that very moment of simultaneous satiation and expiration, there came a knock on the door.

"Mr. President? Everything okay in there?" It was the Secret Service agent assigned to his care.

Still breathing heavily, Evan managed to mutter, "I'm just taking a little breather, Lieutenant Phillips."

"Madame, you alright?" he asked.

"She's asleep," Evan answered. "Long day, you know?"

The man, who had clearly seen both Evan and his mother enter the side room, was evidently curious about what just had taken place. Evan could tell. After a moment's pause, Evan finally heard departing footsteps. Well, however things may have stood during the last administration, this man would need to learn the new ground rules soon, Evan thought. Curiosity on certain sensitive matters would be highly discouraged, in no uncertain terms.

He cast his eye again upon his mother, the woman who had abused him and countless others during her lifetime. Evan knew all about Eveline Agatha Crumple's various projects and what they involved; he knew the relish with which she had attended to her work, the depths of her voracious appetites.

She had, after all, told him everything. He believed himself to be the only person in the world who knew the full extent of Eveline's depredations. She had spoken of her behavior freely, without restraint, to him and to him only.

Tears welled up in his eyes as he beheld the now utterly still form of the woman who had given him birth. How many times had she held him, kissed him, caressed him fiercely and tenderly; how often had they carried forth their forbidden trysts, just out of the eyesight of the world? How young had he been the very first time? Evan found that he could not recall. Had she first seduced him before he was even old enough to remember?

Why then was he now weeping for this monster, this creature who had taken his innocence precisely when she ought to have safeguarded it most diligently? She had made a wreck of him, had twisted him into the foul creature that he had become. She had stripped him of all virtues, had defiled him repeatedly, all for the most perverse of motivations; that is, it had precisely been the reverence she felt for him, a reverence as authentic as it was profound, that had made her wish to plunder the treasure he represented to her, to plunder it so thoroughly and so often.

"*Why,* Eveline...why did you make me have to do that?" Evan began to sob, as full knowledge of the finality of his mother's passing struck him suddenly. He had hated her, but he had also loved her, in a way. He had reciprocated her passion for him with every ounce of his own libidinous fervor. He, unlike she, had been monogamous in his perversity; there had never been any other woman for him but her. But now, she lay dormant, stiff, bleeding from both ends, as a result of his double-pronged assault.

He sobbed for a moment longer, then wiped his eyes and stood.

"You brought me here, Mother. You made me who I am today. You made me a bad man. And I will rule like a tyrant, with an iron fist, just as you trained me to do. But you didn't fully know me, Eveline...I am a bad man, but...I...will...do...good!"

Her mouth, twisted in a death grimace, seemed to express skepticism. He felt her scorn viscerally, as if her spirit, set free, were telling him in no uncertain terms that she detected humbug. *"I know what you're all about,"* he almost heard her whisper. *"Your heart is as black as mine. Like me, you believe in absolutely nothing, except power. You will do what you must to keep and consolidate your power and control."*

He recalled well his mother's tutelage. America, she informed him, had grown weary of globalism, of enforced imperial expansionism pushed by the world's elites, of the loss of their national sovereignty to those eager to install a "one world government" and a "new world order" and a "great reset." The time was ripe, she urged, for a true "populist" leader. Evan must become that leader.

"People have had it," she told him. "They want someone who'll pull out all the stops. They are enraged. They want heads to roll, and not figuratively. Literally! You must *become* that man, the leader who makes their heads roll, who baptizes the birth of a new nation with a bloodbath of the Old Guard!"

His mother spoke from a position of authority; she was, after all, deeply entrenched within the "globalist" conglomerate "Their problem," she had confided, "is that they actually hold to principles! They see their power and control as a means to an end. They are out of touch with the people, because they despise the people, and don't account them as even worthy of consideration...their arrogance will be their downfall, if we play our cards right...

"You must become a man of the people," she had instructed him, as she lay naked next to him in bed one evening, in a typical post-coital rush of insight. "They must see, must understand, that you are *different* from the rest of them...you must *bewitch* them!" Evan had known that when his mother had used the word "bewitch," she hadn't meant it metaphorically. He had inherited unique psychic skills, she told him, and he must use them.

"Harness that potentiality," she had "Your father, may his soul rest in power, lent you this gift. In him, of course, it took a raw form. He was a 'man of wrath,' and the darkness of his spirit, coupled with my indomitable ambition, gave you the power to become the being whom the world is groaning to receive, the king it is dying to crown..."

His mother had undoubtedly made him the man that he was...but had he wanted to be the man she had made him into? He now stood at the pinnacle of world power, but if he'd had his druthers, would he be here, or would he, rather, be living an entirely different life?

Such questions, Evan decided, were idle and best discarded, lest they clutter up his brain with doubt, pain, resentment, and other undesirable emotions. He bent over, pushed his mother's eyes shut.

"I will do *good,*" the murderer insisted one more time to the corpse of his victim, before pulling up his pants, straightening his tie, and nodding to his visage in a side mirror.

When it came to the tricky matter of disposing of the body, Evan knew of only one man who could be trusted with the task. Sitting cross-legged on the couch, next to the body on the floor, he pulled out his phone.

"Julius?" he said. "I need you to come down here now."

Moments later, Julius Ambien, upon entering the room, gasped at the grisly sight.

"My God in Heaven," he muttered breathlessly, clutching at his sides and grimacing in a manner that weirdly mirrored the corpse's twisted mouth death-expression.

Evan, warily noting the older man's demeanor, declared, "If you're gonna throw up, go outside."

"No," answered Julius. "I have seen death before. Many times."

Evan had first met Julius five months ago, when the latter was still in the heat of the presidential race. Eveline had introduced the man—a wan, spectrally thin fellow in his mid-40s—in a quite auspicious manner.

"Son," she had said, "I would like you to meet Julius Ambien. He is a dear old friend. He is here to help you out with anything you might need."

The circumstances of the meetup had been quite strange. His mother had just shown up with this stranger while Evan was coming down the homestretch of the campaign trail. Eveline had been by his side for nearly the entire arduous process, but she had disappeared for a day, returning with this character, who was, in the words of Shakespeare's Caesar, one whose visage betrayed a "lean and hungry look"; indeed, whether or not he smiled, his eyes remained peculiarly fixated upon some seemingly intense and all-important matter, which he apparently wasn't allowed to discuss, no matter how much it plainly preoccupied his mind.

Were Mother and this man...? No, he assured himself, it couldn't be. Evan knew all about Eveline's predilections, of course, but her tastes, predatory as they were, tended to run almost exclusively towards the young. This man, while younger than Eveline, was surely still much too old to interest her in that way. Yet she fawned over him most peculiarly, in a manner that seemed patently flirtatious; she would tease him playfully, touch his arm, even hold his hand. For his part, the man seemed to be made only more uncomfortable by all of her gestures, though he made a halfhearted effort at playing along.

Evan wasn't sure how to feel about this Julius Ambien, or the affections his mother bestowed upon him, or how he reciprocated her attention in a manner that seemed like playacting. He found himself afflicted with a painful bout of jealousy, as he had never witnessed his mother behaving amorously towards anyone else in his presence. Yet he could not escape the suspicion that Eveline had this fellow in some compromising position, and this awareness tempered his perverse impulses.

As the evening wore on, Eveline suggested that the three of them ought to repair to their motel room, as she had "important news of an intimate nature" to impart. Evan attempted to beg off this strange invitation, declaring that he had a long day tomorrow; the final debate was scheduled for the evening, and he needed to go over his notes to ensure the best possible performance. At this, his mother smirked. "Come now, darling," she said. "You have this election sealed up. It is inevitable by this point. Nothing can stop it, nothing *will* stop it. You can spend just a bit of time with your dear old mom and her new man friend, can't you?" She winked, and the matter was settled.

In the elevator to her room, Eveline, in the presence of her "new man friend," suddenly grabbed her son roughly and began kissing him. Evan, only partly shocked by this development, sighed. "Mother, please." She then began grabbing him at his crotch, and to Evan's consternation (but not surprise), he found that could not curb his own arousal, even at this most inappropriate time. Julius taken aback, stared with wide-eyed horror at the turn things had taken.

In her room, she started in on Evan again, and the latter was about to give in again, as it seemed he always did, when Julius suddenly spoke.

"Eveline, stop it now. Stop it! He's your son, stop it!" he shouted. Then he was picking her up and pushing her against the wall. Nonplussed, she merely gazed into his eyes, amused.

"Jealous, *fuckboy?*" she goaded, and he slapped her hard. Evan leapt to his feet, prepared to protect his mother with deadly force, but she laughed and said, "No, son, stay where you are. I deserved that one. I was hoping it was coming, and I wasn't disappointed..." She turned her glance back to Ambien, eyeing him with great awe, the sort of awe that she had always heretofore reserved for her son.

"Oh, man of wrath," she whispered. "Fuck me now. Do it, *right in front of your son!* Rape me, use me the way you did it before..."

Ambien took a step back. his eyes wide. He turned to Evan, whose face had gone utterly expressionless.

"He has entered a fugue state," she declared. "He cannot make the truth match his perception thereof, concerning the fact of his paternity. He will be fine. But while he's out, let me tell you something about yourself, *fuckboy...*"

Ambien felt enraged anew; seizing her by the throat, he hissed, "Do not call me that again!" He flung her to the floor, where she lay for a moment, catching her breath. "The way you are with your son…it's abominable!" he declared. "No mother should..." He broke off, finding himself unable to put to words the horror and disgust he felt for her. She remained recumbent and gazed directly into his eyes.

"Everything I have, I give Evan," she said. "I know you don't understand, but things couldn't be otherwise. Without me, he would never have been shepherded to this pinnacle, where he belongs...I never revered anyone until I gave birth to a god. With gods, different rules apply. You don't have to approve, I don't ask you to...but what about you, *man of wrath?* How do you factor in? Haven't you ever wondered that?"

Julius said nothing, so Eveline, rebounding to her feet, quite boldly stood in front of him again, seemingly unafraid of being smacked in the face or choked in the throat or otherwise harmed by him.

"You were an only child. You parents never understood you. You always felt that they wished you'd turned out differently. Their disappointment with you was palpable, from a very young age. Am I accurate so far?" She brought her face even closer to his, and though her eyes appeared to be filled with compassion, her voice remained hard and ruthless in tone.

"You wondered if you really were born from them, but here is the truth. Are you ready? Your mother, unbeknownst to your father, was an avid esotericist. She always felt, in spite of having married your father, that your dear old dad just wasn't worthy of her."

Julius remembered how his mother, a haughty and distant woman, barely tolerated him. Yet she tolerated his father, a brooding, balding, habitually unemployed alcoholic, even less. Such a circumstance would have caused Julius to feel bonded with his father, had it been for the fact that his father seemed only to resent him for being slightly more favored by his mother than he was.

His father would often insult him, calling him weak, silly, and stupid on numerous occasions, whenever he failed to carry out some task to the level that met with his father's expectations. During the few times when he actually managed to perform in a manner consonant with what his father had expected (whether it be a chore, or a school project, or an athletic task), no praise was forthcoming, just a sullen silence. Though he had, during the bulk of his early years, tried hard to elicit an actual gesture of approval from his dad, he eventually gave this up, seeing that it was clearly no use.

His mother, by contrast, was rarely hostile to him, just chronically indifferent. At time he caught her looking at him with a certain disinterested curiosity, as if he were a toy, with some built-in feature that was expected to manifest itself. His mother would even, it seemed—was he really remembering this correctly?—at times attempt to pit him against his father, almost in the spirit of one running an experiment, interested to observe the outcome.

"Your mother conceived you in a most unusual manner," Eveline said. "She didn't want just *any* child. She had ambitions...she was, I daresay, a woman after my own heart! The difference was, she didn't really know what she was doing...she read a lot of books, and saw mediums. One of these would-be gurus taught her to meditate in a particular manner, to repeat incantations asking that her womb be opened to an 'ascendant master' so that her offspring could be special...of course, it was actually your mother who wanted to feel special...

"But guess what? An ascendant master, the sort of creature that all of those fool Nazarene-lovers out there would call a 'demon,' *did indeed come upon her one evening..*"

At this moment, Julius suddenly found his consciousness transported to a most distressing scene. He saw his mother screaming as some ghastly creature had its way with her. In his mind, the moment wore on and on, never seeming to end. His mother's tormented shrieks only grew more pitched, and she began most pitifully to beg for mercy, to absolutely no avail. The beast which ravaged her only stepped up its efforts, laughing all the while in a manner so horrifying that Julius felt that he might faint from fright. He cried out for the mental image to stop, and presently it did, and his mind was mercifully whisked back to the present.

"Your mother got a bit more than she bargained for," Eveline stated, with just the slightest hint of a malicious grin playing upon her lips. "She is like so many who treat the dark arts as if it were some sort of hobby. She found it was not mere fun and games..."

"I don't believe you, you evil bitch," Julius spat, with a bravado that belied his sinking heart. Fully enraged now, he slapped her again, but she just laughed.

"Of course you don't *want* to believe me," she sneered. "Who wants to accept that he's the bastard child of a demon? But that's you, fuckboy. You are the son of Wrath. The dark spirit who had its way with your mother, it was a demon of Wrath...that is why it tore her apart the way it did on the occasion of your, ahem, conception."

Once more, he was forced to hear his mother's piteous wails as that ungodly abomination tore at her insides in various ways, each more obscene than the last. He doubled over, fell to his knees, screamed for her to make it stop, to get out of his head. He heard a voice, Evan's voice, yell out, "Mother! Stop it, now! Mother, you're going to kill him, stop! *I won't let you hurt him!*"

The horrifying vision ceased at last, and Julius saw that Evan had shaken himself out of his stupor and was extending a hand, palm outward, toward his mother.

"I won't let you hurt him, Mother," he repeated, his voice now even and commanding. She scowled at him for a moment, then returned to the venomous grin she had flashed moments before.

"How touching. A son protecting his father..."

"Shut up," he immediately commanded. She obeyed. He went on, "Mother, you will *not* bring this up again. Mr. Ambien will accompany me for the next two weeks, leading up to Election Day. He is with me from now on. Do you understand, Mother?"

She responded, curiously, with a snake-like hiss; for a split second, it seemed, she seemed to morph into something plainly inhuman, something with discolored skin and ghastly black eyes. Then something even stranger happened; Evan hissed back, louder; for a brief moment, he too seemed to transform into an ungodly entity. It had apparently been a display of dominance, and it had worked; his mother cowered, lowered her eyes.

"Mr. Ambien and I will take our leave now," he said. He strode toward the door and Julius followed, resisting the temptation to look back.

Once the two men were alone, Julius became all business. He apologized for his mother's behavior and said she wouldn't be a problem for him any longer. "I'll make sure she stays away from you," he told Julius.

And so she had.

Ever since that day, a mere three weeks ago, Evan had seen to it that Julius was taken care of, and was kept out of the Eveline's orbit. But the two of them seldom talked during this span of time, and Evan never broached the topic of Julius' alleged paternity. Had he truly entered a fugue state when this was mentioned in his presence, as Eveline had declared, since the notion was just too upsetting to confront directly? Or had he heard, and understood, and was now simply opting to keep the troubling news at a distance from himself?

Whatever the case may have been, Julius decided not to broach the subject again, unless the matter were introduced by Evan himself.

As for Eveline's disturbing claims concerning his own alleged paternity, Julius tried his hardest to shove the very idea from his mind, to purge it from his memory. "She's a *liar,*" he told himself, reminding himself that she possessed the telekinetic abilities to make him see and hear the horrible scene he was forced to witness in his mind's eye and ear, but that this in no way meant that the scene was authentic or true to life or that it had actually happened.

However, when thoughts of his mother's torment came back, as they inevitably did, Julius always felt assaulted by oppressive waves of fear and nausea. He made desperate efforts to distract himself, and luckily, since he now dwelt in the hub of a full-bore presidential campaign heading into its homestretch, there were plenty of available distractions. Yet if he looked too closely into the eyes of the young man who now sheltered him and provided him with succor, out of the hands of his former jailer and tormentor, he could scarcely avoid the selfsame strain of thought which led invariably into a horror which engulfed him and caused him to break out into a fierce bout of flop sweats. For was this very young man, his own son, not, in fact, *also a being of that infernal strain?*

The dots were all there to connect, Julius knew. But he must keep those dots at a distance from himself, somehow, or he might just lose his sanity for good.

Now he stood next to the new boy-president in the small room and beheld the now lifeless body of the woman, the same she-beast who had tormented him for so long. She was bleeding from the nose and mouth, but much more copiously from between her splayed legs; the blood just below her crotch had formed a puddle which was now thoroughly soaking her dress.

Julius, was of course, at a loss. He didn't even ask any questions. What, really was there to inquire about? He knew what had happened, and he knew why. Seeing Eveline dead came as a relief, he found, but also as a shock. She was, after all, the mother of his...child.

"She was justly served," Evan declared, yet not without a sudden spasm of grief. "She was...the only woman I ever..." He stopped short, as if only now realizing how it sounded. A moment later, he managed, "I don't expect you to understand, Julius, but she taught me to be who I am. I wouldn't be where I am without her. I wouldn't understand what must be done, if she hadn't compelled me, pushed and prodded me to be it."

The elder man said nothing, as he was unsure how to respond to this seeming apologia on behalf of a woman who had freely indulged in evil and perverse behavior for nearly the entirety of her adult life. Then, recalling his own violent fantasies with shame and chagrin, acts in which he had indulged freely at this same woman's goading invitation, he realized with a shudder that, in fact, he did understand something of his son's simultaneous sentiments of vindication and anguish.

As if sensing his inner turmoil, Evan now turned to him.

"I enjoin you, Father," he said, "to join me in a solemn pact. What you have seen, what you know, must forever remain a secret. I charge you in the name of the royal blood that we share, in the name of our mutual sacred heritage, to make your allegiance known to me now."

Julius, his mind reeling at the younger man's admission, his sudden imposition of the never-before broached paternity matter, found himself nodding.

"You agree to this pact? If so, swear your solemn fealty to our bond."

"I swear," Julius heard himself saying.

"It is who you are, and it is who I am. You made me who I am just as surely as Mother did."

Had the youth caught the apprehension in his tone, and did he know the torment which now chafed at his heart?

"You are exactly as you were supposed to be," his son informed him. "Everything is exactly where it ever had to be...yes...the Nazarene had his hand in this, too."

Julius's mouth now felt dry as Christ's must have felt as he suffered on the cross, when his tormenters cruelly poured vinegar down his throat.

"Are you...afraid to say his Name?" he dared to ask his son.

"Old habits die hard," he admitted. "All of my life I was taught, by her, that he was the 'Adversary.' I now see things a bit differently. None of what has happened would have happened, had it not been His will. And none of what will happen under my rule will violate his will. It was always meant to be."

Julius looked again at the figure of the dead woman, bleeding so visibly from her womb, the womb that he had only half-wittingly seeded so many years ago in the backseat of that limo. It was a pitiful and appalling sight, yet it seemed to be in many ways the perfect cause of her demise. She who lived for her womb's visitation by a "man of wrath," she who had so loved the seed of wrath that had entered her loins that she transcended all boundaries of propriety, decency, and natural law, descending into even greater levels of depravity than she ever had previously in her abomination of an existence, and all out of allegiance to the powerful being that she had helped to bring to life, had now died due to a wrathful assault upon that very same womb.

She who had lived by her womb, who had in fact continually and gluttonously, and quite scandalously, fed her womb with the very being whose form had first taken shape there, who had worshipped the wrathful power of her son's loins so much that she had forcefully yielded to them on endless occasions, had now found herself undone by the very wrath which had driven her to such appalling extremes.

"She had never once expressed doubt or remorse," remarked her son. "Even up to the very end." He began to weep again, but it was an odd sort of weeping which at times lapsed into peals of truly hideous laughter. "Oh Mother," he whispered. "Are you still without remorse? Are you *still smiling in Hell?*"

Julius let the younger man indulge in his weird spasm of mingled grief and mirth for a moment, but found forever afterwards that this final question would never stop haunting him. If she was still smiling, how truly was cursed that smile, how infernally repulsive must it be to behold!

EPILOGUE

To the prior narrative, I, the curator of this historical narrative, feel that it is necessary to append an epilogue of sorts.

With the remove of years, and with the benefit of hindsight, it is not altogether easy for us to comprehend the state of things as they stood just on the cusp of the era that we now find ourselves fortunate enough to inhabit, an era of peace, in which all governmental officials are held to strict standards of transparency (a gesture naturally and un-self-consciously reciprocated by a loving and reverent populace), a time of prosperity and calm, in which the blighted, benighted sham government called "democracy" has long been ended, and a dynastic ruling family, of whom the now properly titled **Emperor Evan the First** proved to be the first in a long and seemingly never-ending line of "people's emperors"—men and women who, in essence, possess a unique psychic bond towards the governed—has come to rightful rule.

There are now no more indulgences in that garish and grotesque ritual known as "elections," during which the usurper oligarchs had free reign to apply maximum psychic abuse upon their helpless populations. Young Evan put an end to all of that. First, though, he had to take part in the disgusting and degrading act of offering himself as a "candidate" for "president." The motivation for him to do this, however, was, like Christ, to suffer the immense degradation that would surely result if one not "chosen" by those same usurper oligarchs, nevertheless opted to run for the position of what was then called "commander-in-chief," that is, the ruler of what was then called the "executive branch."

Emperor Evan I is now acknowledged, and his memory revered, for possessing royal and divine blood, which in fact meant that he was fit to ascend to rulership as a matter of principle. In truth, he needn't have put himself through the ludicrous, unbecoming, and undignified rigmarole of making himself just one "candidate" among others. But just as Christ's destiny was to masquerade as the lowliest of men, and suffer the humiliation and pain of being put to death like a common criminal through the most egregious of methods of execution ever devised, so Evan the First, also known as Evan the Great, had to tread the path of a "common politician," that most (rightfully) despised of people, when in actuality his rule should never have been contested, as he represented the true bloodline of *legitimate* rulers, those men and women who may be properly viewed as "set apart" from the mass of humanity, as can be attested, again, by the unique psychic bond that unites them to their people and unites their people to them. And just as Christ was raised to glory following his time of trail, so too was our beloved leader, the Son of Hermes, the man of righteous wrath, slayer of the false, underminer of the usurpers, restorer of order and glory.

For centuries, the nation had been laboring under the democratic delusion. The notion that *truth* was dependent on what the majority decided at any given time was, of course, violative of common sense, and ought to have been recognized as such. However, what had been worse was the fact that this said "democracy" was always just a fraud and a smokescreen, and that the usurpers, plunderers, degenerates, and impostors, whose name at the time was Legion, had managed to hide their covert tyranny under the banner of "democracy."

The fact was, the people never were *truly* entrusted to rule themselves. No crucial societal change ever came about due to any "vote." All had been decided beforehand. The only unpredictable aspect derived from the fact that the usurpers belonged to different factions, and it wasn't always sure which faction would prevail at any given time. What was known, however—to everyone truly in the know, anyhow—was that *any* major decision concerning the present and future course of society, culture, or government would be decided not by vote or public referenda, but by the secret machinations of the usurper factions. Sometimes the faction called "right-wing" or "conservative" won out, and other times the "left-wing" or "liberal" faction did, but generally speaking these decisions amounted to little of substance, since, substantially speaking, the oft-squabbling factions in truth always had far more in common with one another than they did with any of the hapless population whom they presumed to rule over.

The usurpers practiced evil in manifold ways, but none more egregious than the cruelties in which they indulged, mostly in secret, against the innocent, particularly children. It is a point of historical irony that Evan the First's mother was one of the most utterly depraved of these creatures. But what set her apart wasn't so much her savagery as her ambition. In the lore which she studied, and which in fact formed the worldview of this clandestine claque of usurping tyrants, she comprehended that a certain "Son of the Suns" would come into being at some point, and would immediately, upon gaining prominence, institute a *rule of wrath,* in which he would gain popular support and acclaim.

Evan's mother sought to be the one who would conceive and bear this being before the world; she fully expected to join him in his rule and to steer it toward what she construed to be the "proper" end of continued tyranny; however, just as the best-laid plans of mice and men often go awry, Eveline's notions of being the true power behind the throne, as it were, with respect to her son, dissolved into dust once the child was born. She immediately forgot her ambitions to control the child, and instead fell into a swoon before him, sensing the immense, preternatural power he represented. It would be no exaggeration, in fact, to observe that her worship of her son was *all-consuming,* igniting her ardor in a manner never heretofore experienced.

That is to say, whenever she engaged in such depredations in the past, especially with children (and all evidence suggests that her appetite was voracious and quite "catholic," in the sense that no one, man or woman, boy or girl, was excluded from being a victim of her feverish libido), which often manifested itself in an egregious manner that could even on many occasions be described as "sadistic," in that it seemed that when victimizing the vulnerable, she took especial pleasure in tormenting and terrifying them.

Upon these occasions, Eveline (who went under the name, both ironic and fortuitous, as "Mother" whilst engaged in secret operations such as those previously described in this narrative), would invariably take the ultra-dominant role, which meant at times engaging in behavior that could certainly be called abusive, often aggravatedly so. Sometimes these indulgences were a part of some clandestine ritual or another (the sordid and shocking details of which I shall spare the reader), and other times simply for "kicks." (As for her husband, the details of whose demise has been recorded elsewhere, there is scant evidence that they ever consummated their marriage; it seems that theirs was exclusively a partnership of convenience.)

As loathsome as Eveline's sexual activities most assuredly were, and as perverse and depraved as her carnal relationship with her own son was afterwards, one must nevertheless note the significance of the shift in her behavior, which was symptomatic of the general change in her attitude.

With previous victims, she had perennially assumed the role of the "dom." But when she began to sexually abuse her own son—it is not clear how young Evan was when this abuse began, and in any case it is a matter perhaps best left to the imagination—she shifted to role of "submissive supplicant." She so revered the boy that she found herself drawn to him in a manner that could almost be described as "reverent." Though her overtures were often aggressive, they also were done in the spirit of one aching for contact with another whom the first felt to be almost a guru, or perhaps even a savior.

It is thus interesting to note that Eveline's own instincts wound up undermining her own "best-laid plans." She had intended to create the "son of wrath" from her very womb with the express purpose of *controlling* the being she had consciously conceived, the better to enhance her own position, as the true "power behind the throne," as it were. Still, once the child had quickened within her, she could not help but view herself as subservient to his will. She attempted to fight this strange new proclivity at first—after all, she had previously been a woman of ruthless, steadfast ambition, who certainly never bowed to anyone, yet when it came to her own son, blood not only of her own blood, but also of the blood of the prophesied "man of wrath," she found herself bowing to his perceived supremacy, and eager to do whatever she could to facilitate his rise to power.

Thus her abuse of the boy, her own child, must be seen in a different light than all of her previous unspeakable indulgences, since with Evan, she, for the first time ever, felt herself *in the presence of one greater than herself.* It was in this very spirit that she welcomed her grotesque demise at his hands, an incident which, as has already been remarked, was brutally fitting, given the life she had led and the means by which she had victimized numberless innocents.

Immediately after gaining the presidency, Evan Crumple was beset with a series of challenges.

Mere hours after he delivered his inauguration speech and murdered his mother (an act that his newly-discovered father, Julius Ambien, helped him to cover up, in coordination with certain other "top men" under his command), a desperate coup was launched by a faction of the military, in conjunction with around half of the members of Congress. Over the course of the following week (in what was to be called the "Seven Days War") in the streets of the capital, President Crumple's loyalists fought, and eventually routed, the insurrectionists.

"This last-ditch effort on the part of these vile traitors to escape justice has been foiled," Evan announced to the nation in a live television broadcast, following the capitulation of his enemies.

Tribunals immediately followed. These trails were quick, and numerous executions by firing squad followed. Thousands of men and women, including those in Congress who had sided with the coup, were marched to a makeshift parapet, then ruthlessly riddled with bullets, before being loaded onto trucks and driven to various mass gravesites across the country.

Crumple decreed the needful dissolution of Congress until an indeterminate time in the future. Then came the public purges of "criminals deep within the bowels of power." (His use of a scatological metaphor here was of course both deliberate and apt.) The new president, after all, knew quite well just who was guilty of unfathomable crimes, and he intended, he said, "to make each and every one of them pay, and pay dearly."

For the length of the following six months, these "criminals" were shackled and marched into various locations—sometimes courtrooms requisitioned for the cause, sometimes larger venues like arenas and stadiums, where they were compelled to reveal the full extent of their heinous acts. Some refused to speak, of course; in such cases, their inquisitor read a litany of their alleged crimes, and victims were brought forth to further attest to the truth of the claims being made.

Given these extraordinary set of circumstances, one would think that the populace would be uneasy. Yet the vast majority of the people fully supported these proceedings, many of them even reveling in the bloodlust fed by the purges, which invariably followed the public confessions of the formerly powerful. For every moment of the proceedings, to be sure, was meticulously covered on television. This fact became especially significant when former television executives and producers were indicted and humiliated before the very medium that had allowed them to thrive and prosper. Similarly, when Silicon Valley titans were brought low, their emotional breakdowns and grotesquely detailed testimonies, in which they duly reported the full extent of their horrific misdeeds, were broadcast all over the internet they had helped to create.

Music and movie executives, producers, and performers were not spared, either. One after another, in sickening succession, they appeared before the "truth committees" and spilled forth a relentless litany of disclosure, confessing openly to some of the most heinous behavior that one could ever imagine, and even, in some cases, well beyond the imagination of even the most hell-stained of hearts or gutter-obsessed of minds.

Widespread shock and revulsion followed these relentlessly queasy confessions, and public demand for further purges escalated. Evan, utilizing the psychic link he possessed with the populace, displayed no mercy, in obedience to the righteous spasm of popular rage. He even denied the besotted any recourse to last-minute recompense, forbidding priests, ministers, and other spiritual counselors from attending any of these now-hated former celebrities and power-brokers in their final moments, and thus cutting off any chance of redemption. "Let them eat fire," declared Evan, in an ingenious rephrasing of the notorious phrase once attributed to the unfortunate Marie Antoinette.

The trials, and subsequent purges, went on for nearly the length of a year. During that time, tens of thousands of formerly highly-placed individuals—whether affiliated with military intelligence, the entertainment industry, the internet, multinational corporations, the medical-pharmaceutical complex, or other formerly "untouchable" entities and organizations—were ruthlessly riddled with bullets. Some met their end with tears and pleas for forgiveness, other with bravado and expressions of defiance, but all met the same ultimate fate at the hands of the new rulers: namely, the triumphant Evan Crumple and his allies.

Critics of Crumple's campaign might have held (though few had the guts to speak these sentiments aloud) that the bloodbath was overly indiscriminate, that more discernment ought to have been applied, that the principle of "innocent until proven guilty" should have been in effect, that the accused ought to have been supplied with attorneys and been given a chance to defend themselves before a jury of their peers. "No doubt many nasty people were indeed eliminated in these purges," they might have said, or at least thought to themselves, "but wasn't this conducted much more like a witch hunt? Might not many of the confessions in fact been induced under compulsion of torture?"

Crumple, for his part, made no effort to address such sentiments, except to declare definitively, "At a time of great evil, it becomes necessary to take extreme measures to restore justice. The demand of justice speaks infinitely louder than the appeal to 'due process.'"

"In any case," he declared, "if, by accident, innocent blood has indeed been spilled, may that blood be upon me and upon my children!"

After the purges came to an end, Evan did not rest; instead, he and his team wasted no time in facilitating a new manner of rule. The country, he announced, would never again be exposed to the trauma and invariable chicanery of a "presidential election." Instead, there would be one ruler, who, though the assistance of his psychic attachment to his people, would promote justice and righteousness, in full concert with those over whom he was given divine charge to rule.

But, he hastened to add, this was *not* to be a dictatorship. For one thing, Evan would respect the inherent rights of citizens as originally enshrined in the Constitution. Unlike the prior regime(s), he would forbid the imposition of campaigns by oligarchical entities with nefarious agendas. Those sorts of people, he added, were eliminated in the purges. Anyone else who felt the desire to attempt to ascend to power "through backhanded and illegitimate means" would soon find themselves meeting the exact same fate as those who were "rightfully purged and stricken from the record of history" for their singularly evil deeds.

Congress, he decreed, would continue to exist, but congressmen and women would no longer be popularly elected; rather, they would be appointed by Evan and his advisors. Of all advisors, the one from whom Evan looked up to most was the man he had met under such strange circumstances, Julius Ambien. Ambien, to be sure, only took to this task with great reluctance, having never imagined himself being one who plays any sort of role with the affairs of state.

Ambien, being the "man of wrath," from whose seed the "rule of wrath," as Evan's early years were characterized, came into being, struggled to reconcile the things he had learned about his genetic composition, which had surely played some role in his identity. On this matter, he was counseled by Evan, the son he had conceived under egregious circumstances.

"You must know that your physical makeup, whatever it may be, even if it be demonic, is ultimately at the disposal of a being far more powerful than any of the demons. If you came into being in such a sordid manner, and I afterwards was created in no less a grotesque way, those are nothing more than facts about our genetic inheritance. But we, too, are creatures of..."

"Of the Most High," Julius answered, aware that Evan, given his perverse upbringing, still hesitated to pronounce his Name.

"...of the Nazarene," he finished, grinning with ironic amusement.

It should also be noted that eventually, the two characters we largely left behind for the latter part of this narrative, the Lilith clone named "one-four-one-zero" and her miracle daughter, named "Beatrix" or "Bea," on account of her being assigned the never before seen identity number of "1410-B" by her handlers, due to her unique identity as the first being to be born of a clone, a bone fide miracle which, as previously explained, took place in spite of her mother having been (like all of her sister Liliths) purposefully constructed without a reproductive system, the better to avoid unwanted complications.

Fourteen and Bea, as they came to call themselves, laid low until the election and the subsequent insurrection were over, then tentatively put out feelers out to the new administration when they felt it to be safe. Julius had never ceased to think about Bea after his kidnapping by the shape-shifting witch known as "Mother," or more commonly, "Eveline Crumple," whose rise and demise has been duly documented here.

The first few nights that he found himself in Eveline's clutches, Julius had prayed fervently for his adopted daughter, and finally he received some kind of indication, floated through the ether, as it were, by the telekinetic and perspicacious Fourteen, that he needn't worry about Bea, that Fourteen, her proper mother, had finally found her, and she was safe and sound.

When the "troubles" had died down, and the long string of purges had finally reached their end, Beatrice and Fourteen finally opted to pay a visit to the Capitol. Bea and Ambien greeted one another with great emotion, while Fourteen, whom Ambien had never previously met, stood by, a bit awkwardly. A moment later, when Bea introduced the woman who was her mother to the man she had always called "Dad," the awkwardness ramified. The two shook hands, but neither could look the other in the eye.

Bea looked from one of them to the other a bit quizzically, unsure what to make of this oddly ticklish moment between the man and the woman. The fact that they had "met" before, in a sense, when Julius received Fourteen's telepathic communique regarding Bea's safety, seemingly did nothing to smooth things over when the two first met in the flesh.

Later, Bea asked Fourteen directly why both of them had behaved so strangely when introduced to one another. To Bea's astonishment, Fourteen had responded by exclaiming, "Did it look like *he* was uncomfortable, too?" as if that was somehow good news, good enough to make this grown woman grin giddily.

Sadly, having been born into the depraved circumstances of the Lilith Lab, neither Fourteen nor Bea had had much interaction with men, or with women, for that matter, which hadn't involved coercion and exploitation. Each had been subjected to unspeakable abuse, and both had accordingly learned to disassociate from their consciousness whenever the prospect of romance or intimacy came into focus. It was all part of functioning as a trained "sex kitten," learning the art of seduction in order to render a "mark" blackmailable.

It had been through the application of such tactics that Fourteen had drawn Dr. Jude Omega into a forbidden tryst, the result of which had been the miraculous—though far from immaculate—conception of Beatrix in the first place. Upon the event of her daughter's birth, however, Fourteen had experienced a thoroughgoing transformation; she had, finally escaped the clutches of that beast known as "Mother," and afterwards tracked down her daughter, aided invaluably by the telekinetic abilities that had been built into her very being, in order to make her a more effective seductress and spy.

Throughout the entirety of her post-awakening existence, after she became aware that Beatrix had miraculously grown inside her and had come out of her body, Fourteen had never experienced what she had just felt when she met Julius Ambien. It had been a queer rush of excitement, a sense of anticipation and nerves. She felt what others afflicted with being "in love" have described as "butterflies," but she did not know this expression, and up to now had never had cause to attempt to grasp this sensation, as it had never previously come over her. Was it pleasant or unpleasant? Somehow it was both, since it threw her off of her even keel, which had previously always been her habitual disposition, even in moments of severe discombobulation.

Beatrix, likewise robbed of a "normal" upbringing which typically involved what were known to normal people as "crushes," was bewildered to see her mother overwhelmed in such a manner. Yet a few hours later, when she met the Supreme Ruler of the reconstituted United States of America—that is, Evan Crumple—she found her own consciousness assaulted in a similarly unfamiliar way. Evan had greeted her with an even stare, and to her considerable surprise, had taken her proffered hand in his and kissed it.

"My father has told me a great deal about you," he said, continuing to keep her gaze, and she became deeply aware of his dark blue eyes. Dear Lord, she thought, those are the eyes of Mother!

Yet despite the terror attendant upon this realization, and the numerous loathsome memories it aroused, Bea found her attention riveted by other aspects of his person: his face, improbably kind and somehow weathered beyond its years, his pronouncedly dominant stature, so much like his father, and the entrancing baritone cadence of his voice, which she had heard many times before on television and the Internet, but which had never struck her as so heartbreakingly vulnerable, suggestive of a man who had never been allowed to be a boy, yet whose boyishness nevertheless wished to make a belated appearance in spite of being kept firmly in check by his better nature.

Bea found herself flooded with a thunderous cacophony of thoughts and emotions and her eyelids fluttered. She felt faint, and feared she might pass out, yet somehow the ecstatic beating of her heart buoyed her up, and she attempted to speak, but could only stutter a series of nonsensical syllables. She closed her mouth, blushed furiously, looked down, then (still looking away to avoid the searing heat of his stare) attempted to speak again, this time succeeding at muttering:

"Your father is also my father."

Then, alarmed at the message this might be conveying, she quickly looked him in the face again, and blurted out, "I mean...he's not my real father. I *killed* my real father."

Evan's eyes widened, and a moment later, he burst out laughing, much to her mortification. Yet he touched her hand again, the same one he had kissed moments earlier, and told her, in a confidential tone.

"My, what a coincidence...I killed my *mother.*"

Now it was her turn to become shocked. Yet almost instantly her shock turned to relief. "You *killed* Mother?" she asked, incredulously, as if the news were simply too good to be true.

"Oh you called her Mother, too?" he rejoined. Yet there was, she found, an oddly mischievous glint in his eye. "You mean we had the same father and the same mother? Dear me, that's a bit awkward..."

Now both Bea and Evan were laughing heartily, as merry pranksters, or inveterate scofflaws might laugh together, in the full intimacy afforded by the realization of being co-conspirators in glorious cahoots.

A mere six weeks after their initial meeting, Evan and Beatrix were wed, in a public ceremony of great pomp and majesty. Beatrix, though 13 years Evan's senior, nevertheless proved to be a perfect match for the young royal. The new queen was loved by her people, who had no idea whatsoever of the hardscrabble life she had led prior to becoming the Emperor's bride.

Nor did the people ever learn the truth about Evan's mother and the obscene depredations which she regularly perpetrated. To the "common folk," Eveline Agatha Crumple had been a loving wife to a heroic senator, tragically cut down in his prime by a wayward, drunken aide, and a marvelous mother to the rising emperor, who ascended to his rightful place as ruler through the ignoble means of election, a practice he afterwards rightly abolished. Mrs. Crumple's unfortunate demise took place just hours after Evan delivered his inauguration speech, and was confirmed by Emperor Evan's personal doctor to be a tragic and untimely heart attack. It was said that, upon seeing her beloved son's ascension to power, Eveline's heart simply "burst for joy."

Following soon after Evan and Beatrix's wedding, albeit with considerably less fanfare, came the "pledging of troths" of the Emperor's chief adviser Julius Ambien and the woman previously known as "Fourteen," who, upon becoming a wife, officially changed her name to "Mary Ambien."

Fourteen, now Mary, derived obvious inspiration for her new name from the prototypical miraculous Mother. Though this Mary knew that she was anything but an "immaculate" woman, she nevertheless felt humbly awed by her namesake, and honored to share in her glory, as yet another mother of a miracle child.

Upon the pair's first act of marital union, as each lay abed, bathed in mutual nuptial bliss, Julius gazed into his gloriously satiated eyes of his happy bride, and realized something at once profound and disconcerting.

"The first time I knew you... in this way," he said, "I found out later that you weren't real."

"That was Lilith," his wife answered. "Lilith is gone. I once was an illusion, but now I'm real. Now I am Mary."

Mere weeks later, the couple received incredible news. Mary, at her now advanced age, was again with child!

Upon receiving these unbelievable tidings, Julius—the man who once bore the title "Man of Wrath"—threw his arms around Mary and wept with a joy so intense it seemed to him scarcely distinguishable from grief.

His wife, her eyes shining brightly, luxuriating in his embrace, smiled beatifically.

"This time," she told him, "it's definitely a boy."

ABOUT THE AUTHOR

Andy Nowicki is a writer, speaker, prophet, seer, revelator, gigolo, assassin, and empath. Former co-editor of *Alternative Right,* Nowicki has contributed to numerous dissident online journals and has published several works of both fiction and nonfiction, including *Considering Suicide, Meta-#Pizzagate,* and *Ruminations of a Low-Status Male.* He lives (for now) in Savannah, Georgia.

terrorhousepress.com

Printed in Great Britain
by Amazon

37902527R00081